A ***COMBATIVE*** NOVEL. BOOK ONE

COMBATIVE

A *COMBATIVE* NOVEL, BOOK ONE

COMBATIVE

JAY McLEAN

COMBATIVE

Copyright © 2015 Jay McLean
Published by Jay McLean

Published: Jay McLean May 2015

1

I FLEX MY fingers, watching the dried blood shift around my knuckles. I should be at home icing the shit out of them, but I'm not. Instead, I'm in a tiny room with nothing but a table and two chairs. I don't know how the fuck I got into this mess. Actually, I do, but the asshole was talking shit and I had no choice.

That's a lie.

There was a choice.

I made mine and I ended up here.

THE DOOR SWINGS open, and a suit walks in—his back to me—talking heatedly with someone on the other side of the door. "I'll handle it, Pulver," he states before slamming the door and then... *nothing*. He simply stands there staring at the closed door, his head shaking. After a moment, he faces me.

The corners of my lips lift the second recognition hits but drop just as fast when he jerks his head. The action's so slight; if I weren't focused on him, I would've missed it. His gaze shifts to the camera in the corner of the room—a split-second movement—but one I understand. Rolling up the sleeves on his crisp, white shirt, the man takes the only seat available on the other side of the table. With his forearms on the table, he leans forward. "Parker."

I smirk. "Officer."

"*Detective*," he corrects, a justified cockiness to his tone.

I don't take the bait. Instead, I mumble, "Who'd have thought."

His features falter but only a second before his mask is back in place. Looking down at the folder in front of him, his eyes scan the page from side to side before his gaze lifts. "Kyler Parker?" he asks, but he already knows who I am.

I nod once, giving nothing away.

His eyes fix on the cuffs digging into my wrists. After letting out a slow exhale, he leans to one side and shoves his hand in his pocket, revealing a set of keys. The second he removes the cuffs, there's a banging on the door. His eye-roll makes me chuckle.

Another suit, a fatter one, stands at the door with his eyes narrowed. "Davis," is all he says.

Davis stands, walks to the door and without a word, proceeds to forcefully shut it in fat-suit's face. Once he's settled back in his seat, he resumes his position from earlier. "You're in a bit of a mess," he states, pulling a picture from the folder and pushing it under my nose. "You recognize him?" My gaze drops to the picture but quickly shifts, the image making my gut twist. My nod is all Davis needs to continue. "You broke his jaw, his nose, busted a rib, and punctured his lung. You also did some heavy damage to his right eye. They don't know if it will have full functionality again." He raises an eyebrow. "Was it worth it?"

I clear my throat and lean forward, matching his position. I don't say a word.

Amusement fills his eyes. "Are you mute?"

I bite my lip to stop from smiling, and the taste of my

blood hits my tongue. He smirks, jerking his head toward my lips. "Does it taste like victory?"

I drop my chin to my chest and do my best to keep it together. The scraping of his chair grabs my attention. He's on his feet now, working his way over and stopping next to me, where he takes a seat on the edge of the table. "Ky," he starts, then pauses for what I assume is dramatic effect. "I can call you Ky, right?" He doesn't give me a chance to answer before adding, "Here's the thing. Witnesses say that you had to be pulled off of him, and even then you kept throwing blow after blow. The damage you did, there's too much of it. Obviously he's pressing charges, as is the owner of the bar you just trashed because you couldn't control your temper."

"Fuck you," I murmur. It's the first thing I've said since he's walked in.

He raises his eyebrows before clearing his throat and crossing his arms. "I could just leave you here. You could go to court—do the whole trial thing. I bet you think your chances of getting let off are high: ex-combat vet suffering PTSD... all that shit. But the truth? The truth is it might've worked if we were talking assault, but we're not. We're talking attempted murder, Parker."

I lean back in my chair and look up at him.

"I'm here to make a deal—one that you should take." With a sigh, he drops his head before pushing off the table. Reaching into his back pocket, he pulls out a pair of handcuffs; the same ones I was wearing when he walked in. He circles them around my wrists—looser than they were before. "You have one night." He places his business card in my hand. "An officer will tail you. I suggest you get a drink and think about taking the deal."

"Fuck your deal."

He smiles openly for the first time. "*Fuck your life*."

2

Officer Declan—the poor asshole chosen to babysit me—hasn't moved from his spot in the last two hours. I flip the business card between my fingers and eye it curiously.

Detective Jackson Davis, right above the Philadelphia Police Department logo.

And his hand-written note: *meet me at Colton's Bar.*

"Asshole," I mumble under my breath.

"I'm the asshole? You're the one who left and never looked back."

I flinch in my seat—not from him being here, because I expected that, but because of the harshness of his words. "Jackson," I greet, watching him take the barstool next to mine.

"I thought for sure you'd at least call. I didn't expect much, maybe a *'hey bro, I'm alive.'*"

I look over my shoulder for Officer Declan, but he's no longer there.

"I told him to leave," Jackson states, getting comfortable in his seat. "So, I'm glad you actually read my note instead of trashing it like I thought you would."

I dip my head and stare at the beer in my hand. "You said something about a deal?"

After ordering a beer for himself, Jackson turns to me. "I need your help."

I don't respond. I don't know how to. I was already fucked, but whatever he's offering isn't going to save me. It's going to save *him*.

It takes a moment for him to answer. "It involves you."

My gaze snaps to his. "What the fuck are you talking about, Jax?"

Running a hand through his hair, he takes a sip of the beer just handed to him. "This stays in the vault. You got it?"

"Sure. Whatever."

"I'm working on a case. It's an underground fighting organization, but we suspect it's more."

"More?"

"We think it's a cover for a drug ring."

"So where do I come in?"

"I need you to fight."

"I don't fight."

"Pretty sure that guy you just put in the hospital would say otherwise." He blows out a heavy breath. "What the hell did he say to get you so amped?"

My jaw clenches, my fingers curl, gripping the beer tighter. "He said the war was fake and that we were fighting for a cause that didn't exist." I search his face, waiting for him to tell me how stupid I was, but it never comes. After a while I add, "I fought so he could wake up every day and not be afraid to leave his fucking house and he thinks—"

"You should've killed him."

I shrug. "Maybe."

"So?"

"So what?"

"Deal?"

I have no real information on what the hell the deal entails, but that's not important. What's important is *why*. "Why?"

His eyes turn to stone. "They're selling shit to *kids*. And when I say shit, I mean *shit*. It's like ecstasy on crack or vice versa."

"And how does that involve me?" I ask, even though I already know the answer.

"Because, Ky, I think it's the same shit that killed Steve."

KY: AGE FOURTEEN

"EVERY DAMN DAY," I mumbled to myself. I dropped my backpack and slowly walked over to the playground. Every day I'd walk past and see the same thing going on—two kids beating the shit out of someone. Normally, I'd walk away and ignore it. Yet there I was—a few steps away from them—and I'd had enough of their crap.

"We know you have money, you little shit!" one of them yelled.

"I don't!" their victim squealed.

Every.

Damn.

Day.

"Give it to us, you pussy!"

One of the bigger guys kicked the kid already on the ground. It must have been pretty hard because he yelped and shouted, "Here! Just take it!"

I crossed my arms and pushed my chest out. "Hey! Leave him alone!"

In sync, the two bullies turned around, eyes already narrowed. "Stay out of it, Parker. This has nothing to do with you!"

I recognized the tormentors from school. They were twins, two years older than me. Harry and Barry Berry. Clearly their parents were just as stupid as their spawn.

The poor, beaten kid slowly came to a stand, patting down his clothes as he did. He had a busted lip and a cut on his cheek. "It's okay, Ky, just go home," he told me.

"Yeah, Ky, just go home!" Barry mocked.

I eyed Barry and his brother, wondering if I could take them both. Luckily for me, my growth spurt hit at twelve. I was tall but not that built. Not that it mattered. I'd grown up around this shit my entire life. I took a step forward and raised my chin. "No."

"What are you gonna do? Fight us both?"

The beaten kid got between us, becoming my shield like he could somehow protect me. He couldn't even protect himself.

"Just stop," he said to me. Then to the others: "I gave you my money. You can leave now."

"No," I cut in. "Give him back his money!"

Barry stepped forward, his stance matching mine. "Or what, Parker?"

His fist was halfway to my face before I reacted by ducking and charging his stomach. The immediate impact on my shoulder made me want to scream out in pain, but I didn't let it show. I didn't even show it when Harry came at me while Barry and I were on the ground. He started to bend over to get me off his brother, but I kicked the back of his knee hard enough that it gave out. Their victim screamed and charged over to Harry, grabbing a backpack on his way, and started beating him with it. I got two punches to Barry's gut before I had a chance to look at Harry—now cursing and lying on the ground, trying to defend each consecutive hit of the backpack.

With my fists balled around Barry's collar, I seethed, "Give him his money back, and while you're at it, give him all of yours!" Next to me, Harry groaned. I laughed. "You too, asshole!"

"Fine!" Barry said, his hand already in his pocket.

Harry cursed again. "Okay!" he yelled. "Just get this psycho off me."

I watched the kid get one more hit in before letting out a maniacal laugh. Standing up, I took the money they were more than willing to hand me and watched them run away.

"You didn't have to do that, Ky. I was handling it," the kid said quietly.

I kept my eye-roll to a minimum when I handed him the money. "What's your name?"

"Jackson," he told me. "I live next door to you."

I shrugged, avoiding eye contact. "I'm sorry I don't know you," I said lamely.

"It's cool. I don't expect you to. I guess it's just kind of hard not to know you."

WE WALKED HOME in dead silence, only stopping when I got to my gate. "So this is me..." I looked over at my house, sure that it had changed a lot in the two years since we'd moved in. Back then, it was a picture-perfect suburban home. Now—the word shithole wouldn't even cover it. It was exactly the kind of house you'd expect someone just like my dad and his pathetic friends to occupy. At first, the neighbors called the cops because the loud music and the general sound of assholeness never stopped. The cops came around a few times, but they never did anything. After a few months, the number of bikes in our front yard outweighed the number of residents that lived on the street. I guess they had no choice but to put up with his shit.

Just like I did.

My front door burst open and my dad walked out—shirtless, tattoos on display—scratching his nuts, his eyes narrowing as soon as he saw us. "Perfect," I whispered sarcastically.

"Well, if it isn't the useless cunt!" Dad yelled.

Jackson shook his head, his eyes cast downward as he fiddled with the straps of his backpack. He waited until he heard the front door close before looking up at me. "So that's your dad?" he mumbled.

I rocked back on my heels. "That's him."

After shoving his hand in his pocket, Jackson pulled out the money provided by the twins. "You should take this."

I waved him off. "Nah." *He lifted my hand and placed the scrunched up cash on my palm. I stayed frozen in my spot, not sure how to respond. Pity—especially from him—was the last damn thing I wanted.* "I'll see you around, Jackson." *I started to walk away, but he grabbed my arm.*

"What are you doing now?" *he asked.*

I looked at his hand on my arm, then to my front door. "Probably getting my ass beat." *I scoffed.* "Again."

"Maybe we should both use this money. We earned it, right?"

WE WALKED TO *the closest diner and ordered everything we could afford—the splurge made even sweeter because of how we obtained the funds. We talked about movies and TV shows. Turned out, he was only a year younger than me, though I would've sworn by his physical appearance and the way he acted that he was no older than ten. After a few minutes of us eating, he rested back in his seat with a huge grin on his face.*

"Did you enjoy that?" *I asked.*

"Yup!" *He nodded enthusiastically.* "You want to know why?"

"Why?"

"Because it tastes like victory."

3

JACKSON DOESN'T OFFER small talk or even a greeting when I show up at the station the next morning. He leads me to the same room as the night before and motions for me to sit down. Then he removes his jacket, takes a seat, and pushes a picture under my nose. "Nate DeLuca," he says.

I lift the picture for closer inspection. It isn't a mug shot; it's a surveillance shot, and from what I can see, there's absolutely nothing remarkable about the guy. Dark hair displayed under his ball cap, average build, around the same age as me —maybe a couple years older. That's basically all I can make out. "And?" I ask.

"And he's who you need to get close to. He runs the fights, but like I said, we suspect it's a cover-up for the drugs. You need to get to know him. You need to live and breathe him. And if you can do that—get in his circle, get in his head— then it can lead us to the people responsible for Steve—" He cuts himself off and looks down at the table, realizing the mistake he was about to make. "For the deaths..." he corrects himself.

"And what do you get out of it?"

"Justice."

* * *

THE FIGHTS, JACKSON told me, are held in basements of bars throughout Philly. You can buy your way in with a five grand VIP membership. The memberships were limited to two hundred. You show up and act like a dick, your membership's revoked.

The venues are announced to a maximum of only sixty people, chosen randomly via text message two hours before fight night begins. In order to get into the basements, you needed to meet somewhere off-site first, show the message on your phone, text it back to a number, and they mark it off a list.

Obviously, Jackson had prepared all of this in the few days since I'd agreed to *The Deal*.

I did everything that was asked of me, and now I find myself standing in the basement of a bar I'd never stepped foot in before. The place is exactly how I imagined—tiny room with barely enough space to move. The crowd's rowdy but obviously interested enough in the fights that they'd fork out five grand just to watch.

I don't watch the fights. I watch the crowd, hoping for a glimpse of a man I've never met before. The man whose life I'm about to ruin. His name—*Nate DeLuca*—repeats in my head over and over, playing hostage in my mind. I have to live and breathe him; that's what Jax said. And that's what I plan to do.

Because Jax isn't just some newbie detective.

He isn't even an old friend.

Jax is my brother.

KY: AGE FIFTEEN

Mayhem ensued in my house while I sat on the roof, again. I'd been in bed for over an hour before finally throwing the covers off and accepting that sleep would be impossible. Holding my arm close to my chest, I maneuvered my bedroom window open and climbed out onto the roof, ignoring the sudden outbreak of goosebumps pricking my skin. I wondered for a moment if he'd managed to dislocate my shoulder this time or just separate it. Tonight's reason for my beating —Dad was drunk. That was it. There were also people over. Him, combined with alcohol plus an audience, always made for a good time for everyone.

Everyone but me.

Even though I was big for my age, I was no competition for him. Give it a year, it might have been a different story. But even if I could've taken him, I sure as shit wouldn't try. It'd make me just as bad as him, and the last thing I ever wanted to is to become him.

Sitting down slowly, I rested my arms on my bent knees and looked up at the stars.

"I wish I may, I wish I might," I whispered, then laughed. "Fuck your wish."

"Ky!" Jackson was half hanging out his window, his hand waving from side to side.

"What's up?" I asked, not lifting my head. I didn't want him to see the freshly swelled bruises around my eyes. Or the cut on my jaw. Or the fact I was a pussy and hiding out from my dad.

From the corner of my eye, I saw his mouth move a few times, probably unsure about what to say—or ask—especially since he most likely knew the answers. Finally, he yelled, "You want to come over? I got the new Halo on Xbox."

I didn't respond with words, but I slowly came to a stand, careful not to move my shoulder, as I dusted off my jeans that were at least three sizes too big. He told me to meet him at his back door, and a minute later I was there, hands in my pockets as I tried to settle my uncontrollable shivers.

He led me up to his room and handed me a hoodie that was way too big for him. I eyed it suspiciously. That made him laugh. "It's an NYU sweatshirt, my dad's way of pushing me to go there. It won't fit me for years." I pulled it over my head and then sat in front of his TV, my eyes cast downward the entire time. He sat down next to me, handed me a controller, and finally said, "You played before?"

I shook my head, my gaze fixed on the controller in my hand. And then I chuckled, the sound surprising to my own ears. "I don't think I've ever seen one of these before."

We spent the entire night playing Halo until the sun came up. In that room, in that one night, we became the most unlikely of friends. Not because he was some kid trying to save me or because I was a kid that needed saving... or even the other way around. We became friends because, in between the few words spoken, the few laughs we shared, and the few times we lost control of those laughs, we saw each other for what we were—just boys that liked to laugh and shoot the shit out of our enemies in an overdramatic video game.

I named his character "Captain Victory."

He laughed and named mine "Captain Combative."

From then on, I spent most nights sleeping on his bedroom floor. He offered me his bed, but I refused every time. Sleeping on the hardwood floor was a shit ton better than what I'd been used to.

A few months later, I came over and there was a bunk bed in his room. I asked him where he got the money. He told me he'd taken up beating on scrawny, defenseless kids and stealing their lunch money as a hobby.

By then, I'd met his parents a few times, mostly when we hung out at his house after school. His mom was always home, and they'd wait until his dad, Jeff, got home from work to settle down for dinner. His mom, Christine, would ask me to stay and have a meal with them. I'd always politely decline, feeling too out of place with Jackson and his picture-perfect family. At night, I'd be in and out of their house while

Jeff and Christine were asleep—or at least, we all pretended it was that way. But every night I'd come over and Jackson would pull out a plate of food from the fridge and heat it up. "Leftovers," he'd tell me.

Then, one night, everything changed.

The night of my sixteenth birthday.

It took everything I had just to make it to his back door.

I'd never asked for help before—but that night, I needed it.

Because that night, I needed to get the fuck away from my dad. If I didn't—I was positive he would've killed me.

I didn't even think about how it would affect them.

I should have thought about it.

I made a fist and pounded on their back door. "Jackson!" I tried to scream, but the knot in my throat prevented it. I looked over my shoulder, watching, waiting for my dad to appear from the darkness.

Jackson's parents didn't fake ignoring it that time. Heated words were exchanged over the thudding of footsteps down their stairs. Relief washed through me, but it wouldn't have shown. I was too far gone—too physically hurt to do anything but use the door to support my weight.

The door opened and Jax was there, his eyes wide as he took in my state. Too weak to stay upright, I fell forward. First to my knees, then the rest of me followed. Even though I'm sure it happened quickly, the fall felt eternal.

I winced in pain as I folded over myself, the one eye I managed to open caught sight of my blood pooling on their kitchen floor. "I didn't know," I moaned, but speaking just made the pain worse; I let out an agonizing cry. Jackson squatted down next to me, his eyebrows drawn in concern. He offered a hand to help me up, and when I finally could, I stood in front of Jax and his parents, my shoulders slumped, my breaths ragged, caused by the blows my lungs had just copped. I choked on the blood filling my mouth—coughing and spurting—feeling the warmth of it trickle down my chin. I heard a gasp and tried to settle my breathing—tried to push my shoulders back—but my body didn't allow it. I eyed them all one by one, pleading for some-

thing. Anything. I needed help. So I asked for it. "Help." And as soon as the single word left my mouth, my body tensed, as if somehow sensing his presence.

The asshole's voice filled my ears. "Don't run away from me, you little cunt. Face it like a man!" At the time, I'd never been more frightened than I was those few seconds before I turned around and faced my dad. Dad—the epitome of someone who's supposed to love and protect you. But he wasn't any of those things. He was the devil. In the flesh. His red-rimmed eyes held so much rage, and when the snarl pulled on his lips and he took a step forward, I somehow stood my ground. His eyes narrowed at Jackson and then at the blood pooled by my feet. Finally, his gaze settled on me. "Useless, weak, pathetic little cunt," he spat out. He took another step forward, his eyes never leaving mine, then his fist rose... The word "stop" reverberated in my ears, and I had no doubt it came from Jackson.

A sound echoed through the house—the unquestionable 'click click' of a pump-action shotgun.

"You best be leaving now," Christine said, her tone full badass. If she was scared or intimidated by the situation, the clarity in her voice completely hid it.

Her name was a whisper as it fell from my lips.

Jeff stepped up beside me.

"Now!" Christine clipped.

The cold steel of the gun barrel pushed against my bare arm as she nudged me to the side and got between the devil and me. "I'm not afraid to pull the trigger," she said, her voice calm. She pointed the gun until it made contact with his chest. "Test me," she challenged. Like she really, really wanted an excuse to pull the trigger and end him.

Slowly, his hands went up in surrender, his eyes moving from her to me.

"Take one more look at your son," said Christine. "Because this is the last time you'll ever fucking see him."

4

"You looking to get eighty-sixed from here?"

I snap out of my thoughts and look up at the man standing in front of me. Shaved head. Black suit. Arms crossed over his huge chest. Fatter than a motherfucker. Wondering for a second why he chose me out of all the people here to approach, I clear my throat. "Who do I need to speak to about fighting?"

He eyes me up and down, slowly, and then he laughs—this all-consuming, guttural laugh. "You and all the other punks," he states. "Watch the fights. We'll talk at the end if you still want in." He grasps my shoulders and makes me face the cage. And I'm glad I do because my initial assumption was wrong; the guys in the cage aren't amateurs. It's clear from their appearance that they're in the same weight class, and I can tell just from watching that their expertise in martial arts is completely different. The cage itself isn't an octagon like most MMA organizations. It's round, which makes it harder for the fighters to corner their opponent and pound them.

The bell dings to signal the end of the second round, and a medic comes in to check on both fighters. The breaks are short but long enough that the fighters can catch their breaths. And just as quickly as it ends, the final round begins.

The fighters bump their glove-covered fists and circle each other a few times before the first punch is thrown. The bulkier fighter uses fancy footwork and quick jabs to keep his distance. He throws a mean right hook, dropping his opponent to the ground. He sees his opportunity and rushes the dude, now lying on his back on the mat. He tries to finish him with some decent ground and pound, but his opponent's good on the ground. Too good. Most likely trained in wrestling or jiu-jitsu. His opponent recovers quickly and catches him in a classic arm bar, but the dude doesn't tap. The crowd screams for him to tap the fuck out, but his pride wins out and his arm snaps.

He'll be out of commission for months.

Stupid.

The loser nurses his broken arm out of the cage and down a clear path into another room.

"Idiot," a voice says from next to me. "He should've tapped the second his arm was locked." I look to my right and come face to face with Nate DeLuca. I try to stay calm on the outside. Inside, my pulse is raging. He asks, his tone flat, "Tiny tells me you want to fight?"

"Tiny?"

"Yeah," He jerks his head to the guy who approached me earlier. "That's Tiny." He waits for me to respond, and when I don't, he adds, "Meet me up at the bar tomorrow, 1400 hours, soldier."

I narrow my eyes at him.

He motions his head toward my chest. "Your dog tags," he says, before patting my shoulder twice and walking away. He weaves through the crowd, hands in his front pockets as if he doesn't have a single fucking care in the world. Too bad for him—I'm about to change all of that.

5

I'M USED TO wearing an ambiguous mask. Which helps, especially when Nate DeLuca walks into the bar and takes the stool next to mine. "You want to fight?" are his opening words.

I nod and focus on the row of bottles lined up behind the bar.

"It takes months," he adds.

"For what?"

"You saw the fights, right? They're not amateurs. Months of training just to get looked at and even longer of showing up to every fight, getting to know the process, the competition... getting to know *me*... building that trust..."

Perfect. "You think I'm untrustworthy?"

"Here's the thing," he starts, turning on his stool to face me. "Normally, we see the prospective fighters around on fight nights. They watch, they learn, and after a while they get the balls to ask what they need to do to get in that cage. You? You show up out of nowhere, and you just *ask*."

My eyes lock with his. "I want to fight."

"Why?"

"Why?" I repeat.

"Yeah. *Why?*" He sighs and rubs his jaw. "Why do you want to fight?"

I give him an answer I know will intrigue him. "Because if I don't beat someone's ass in a controlled environment I'll end up killing someone. That's why." And with that, I stand up, throw some cash on the bar and head for the door.

"Wait for the text," he shouts.

Passing Tiny on my way out, I raise my hand to let DeLuca know I've heard him.

I wait until I've walked a few blocks before calling Jackson, and he tells me to meet him at my apartment. I almost ask how the fuck he knows where I live, but then I remember who he is now and a knot forms in my stomach, slowly releasing the guilt I've been repressing for years.

I should've been there.

I should've known the man he'd become.

KY: AGE SIXTEEN

FOR DAYS AFTER my sixteenth birthday I refused to talk about what happened. Jax's parents walked on eggshells around me. Christine tried to make me feel as at home as possible, but it was hard. I wasn't used to the attention, and I didn't know how to act. After a few nights of Jackson tiptoeing around me, I finally caved and confided in him. "My dad found out I wasn't his," I told him, sitting on the edge of the bottom bunk.

"You didn't know?" he asked.

I took one more look at the framed picture of Jackson and me sitting on his bookshelf. Then I let out a bitter laugh. How did I not know? I glared intently at myself in the picture, smiling... dimples on show, my blue eyes reflecting the sunlight. Neither of my parents had dimples or blue eyes. I shook my head as I answered, "He beat the shit out of Mom and me. Mom got in her car and took off. She just left me there, Jax. She left so that he could take it out on me. Steve doesn't know."

"Who the hell is Steve?"

"My brother," I said incredulously, like he was a dumbass for not knowing. "Or half-brother, I guess."

His eyes bore into mine. "I've known you for over a year now, Ky. I've never seen this Steve guy around, and you've never mentioned him. Not once."

With a shrug, I said, "He couldn't put up with Dad's bullshit and left years ago. He used to come around to check on me..." I cleared the lump in my throat. "He wasn't there to protect me. And I'm not even mad because I should be able to protect myself."

"You're a kid," Jax said, "It's not your job to protect yourself. Especially from your family."

"But they're not..." I sighed out.

"Not what?"

"My family. I have none."

He sat down next to me, his tone matching mine when he said, "We're your family now, Kyler."

6

JACKSON BARELY STEPS foot in my apartment before doing a slow turn in the middle of the living room, hands in his pockets and his gaze everywhere at once. "This is—"

"It's enough," I interrupt, walking to the kitchen and pulling two bottles of water from the fridge. I lift one in offering, but he shakes his head. Moving on from his appraisal of my furnishings, or lack thereof, he takes a seat on the couch. "You probably have to train now, right? I mean, throwing punches at drunken assholes is one thing—but being in a competition..." he trails off.

"I'll handle it." I lean back on the kitchen island and stare at the back of his head, wondering how the hell it is I got myself in this mess.

"So you're fighting soon?" he asks, half turning to me.

"No. He said I needed to see a few more fights, get to know the process, get to know him..."

He smiles. "That's perfect." He pulls a phone out of his pocket and throws it at me.

"What's this?" I ask, looking at the phone now in my hand.

"Your new phone. Department issued. We can listen in on your calls and track you."

"Are you fucking kidding me?"

"This isn't a walk in the park, *Parker*." He grins. "Oh, and there's something else," he says, scratching his jaw. "The department needs you to do one more thing."

"What now?"

He sucks in a breath with a hiss, and I already know I'm going to hate what he says next. "Anger management therapy."

I scoff. "You and your department-issued phone and therapy can fuck off."

He shrugs lazily, but I can already see his confidence fading. "Looks like jail time for you then," he says, standing up and making his way to the door, pausing when his hand covers the knob. "Call Mom."

My gaze snaps to his. "Did you tell her I was back?"

"And have to deal with the wrath of my mother? Fuck no. I'm good. But don't be a dick, Ky—call her." I stay silent. "I'm serious, man." He swings open my door and gives me one last disapproving look.

A second later, a text comes through on my non-department-issued phone.

DeLuca: *All my fighters train at Xtreem MMA gym. Be there in ten. Gunner's your man.*
Ky: *Got it.*

* * *

Ky: *Got a text from DeLuca. I'm training at Xtreem MMA gym. It's only a block from me. He says it's where all 'his' fighters train. I kind of hate this guy already. I'll be there in ten. Call you after.*

Jackson: I know the one. We've seen him go there a few times. Thanks.

Jackson: By the way, I'm sorry about the therapy thing, but it's out of my hands. Who knows? It might do you some good. I've made an appointment with the therapist. Trust me. You'll like her.

* * *

I WASN'T EXPECTING to see DeLuca at the gym—but here he is. So, too, of course, is Tiny. I bump fists with him as I enter, attempting to build some form of camaraderie. He jerks his head in a nod and continues his stance, arms crossed over his fat gut.

"You his bodyguard or something?" I ask, motioning toward DeLuca.

"Something," Tiny answers, his deep voice lacking any trace of humor.

My gaze moves back to DeLuca—his eyes squinted, focused on a laptop on the table in front of him. He's leaning on his forearms, rubbing his chin as his eyes move from side to side.

"Boss Man," Tiny shouts, and DeLuca's eyes snap up. He smirks when he sees me, shuts the laptop, and carries it over to Tiny, who locks it securely in a briefcase. DeLuca pats me on the shoulder like we're old fucking friends. "I hope you don't mind. I like to keep all my fighters in one place. That way I know who I can trust."

"Whatever." I shrug. "Just tell me what I need to do to fight."

Tiny's chuckle has us both turning to him. "Sorry, Boss," he says, a slight smile in place. "The kid's hungry. I like it."

DeLuca's eyes trail back to mine, his head tilted to the side. He assesses me a moment before smiling. "Me, too,

Tiny. Me, too." He shoves his hands in his pockets and takes a few steps toward the cage in the middle of the gym. "Let me introduce you to Gunner."

* * *

GUNNER IS, WITHOUT a doubt, a hundred percent focused on training. He quickly makes it known that DeLuca's his boss, and he's paid to train me. Nothing more. Nothing less.

Which is perfect.

He tells me I'll be training five days a week. Three of those days will include two sessions.

He's good at what he does. Really good. Even after only one sparring session, I can tell that my fists and the hand-to-hand combat training the army provided aren't enough to get me through my first fight. With a drunk at a bar? Maybe. But not with a professional. I have a lot of work to do. And not a lot of time to do it.

> **DeLuca:** *How'd your first session go?*
> **Ky:** *Fine.*
> **DeLuca:** *Good.*

I call Jackson, who answers on the first ring. "How was it?"

"Fine."

"Get anything?"

"You're gonna have to either give me some time or at least some pointers, because—"

"Just tell me what it was like... how many people were in there?"

"A couple coaches, same number of fighters, DeLuca and his bodyguard, Tiny."

"They were there, too?"

I open the doors to my building and stop in my tracks. "Yeah," I answer, distracted by the brunette standing in front of the mailboxes, kicking the shit out of the wall and cursing.

"What were they doing?" Jax asks.

"I'm going to have to call you back."

MADISON

FOOTSTEPS BEHIND ME come closer and closer, causing my heart to race and my hands to shake. I do my best to turn the key in the lock—praying I can get inside before whoever it is can get to *me*. I twist left. Nothing. Right. Nothing. "Fuck."

I feel his presence beside me before I see them. "Do you need some help?" a deep male voice asks, his tone genuine, not at all intimidating as I'd feared. I relax my shoulders, hoping to seem somewhat normal, and when I finally turn to him, clear blue eyes stare back at me. His smile falters a moment before he goes back to showcasing the deepest dimples I've ever seen. "Yeah," he says, taking a step closer, his huge frame covering me. "You definitely need help."

"I-I can't get this open," I stammer, my breath caught in my chest.

He covers my hand with his, and I do everything I can to hold still. To not pull away. To not punch him in the dick like I'd been told to do if I ever feel uncomfortable. He moves both our hands to the box on the left. "That's because you're trying to open mine."

My cheeks flame with embarrassment. "Sorry."

He shrugs and rests a shoulder on the wall, his gaze lowered as he shoves his hands in his pockets. "Are you new... in the building, I mean. You're my new across-the-hall neighbor?"

"I guess," I tell him, pretending to be occupied with the

content of my empty mailbox. After shutting it, I force myself to look at him. "I'm Madison."

He smiles and nods but doesn't speak, so I take it as my cue to leave.

I make it to the elevator doors before he stops next to me. We wait, pretending to be focused on the numbers above the door. He breaks the silence first, "I'm Ky."

Ky.

The doors open and I step in. He doesn't—what he does is stare. Right at me. I swallow nervously. "Are you coming up?"

He murmurs a "Yup" as he steps inside. We spend the ride to the third floor in complete silence. When the doors open, he rushes out and holds them in place, waiting for me to get out... which I do—because I'm not eighty; I can get out of an elevator just fine. Still, I smile at him, no matter how fake it may look, and he smiles back, just as fake. So here we are— two strangers standing in the hall, smiling stupidly at each other.

"Bye!" he almost shouts, walking past me to his apartment opposite mine.

Great, I think to myself. First person I meet out in the real world and he may be crazy.

I enter my apartment and sit on the couch, then proceed to stare at the wall.

I don't know what to do. Or where to go. The freedom's too overwhelming.

Madison: *I met a Ky.*
Sara: *Good.*
Madison: *I miss you.*
Sara: *Me too.*

7

KY

PULLING MY EYES away from the certificates hanging on the wall, I look back at my therapist, my brow bunched. "Is that your real name?"

She smiles, and I can immediately tell why Jackson found it necessary to tell me that I'd like her. She's in her late twenties with bleached-blond hair and the type of leathery skin that hinted she spent way too much time in the sun. Her tits are *huge*. Fake, but huge. She's hot... if you were sixteen and didn't have any standards... or if you were Jackson, apparently.

Her bright red lips curve higher as she looks over at me, making a show of uncrossing and recrossing her long legs. She squares her shoulders, I suppose as an attempt to maintain some form of professionalism.

I look away.

She finally answers. "My parents were on crack," she says, an amused lilt to her tone.

"Cinnamon Aroma?" I raise an eyebrow. "That can't be real."

"I couldn't make that up if I wanted to."

I kick my legs out and slump further into the chair.

She clears her throat. "So why are you here, Ky?"

"Isn't it your job to tell me that?"

"Do you want to be here?"

With a sigh, I roll my eyes and sit up a little. "I'm sure you know why I'm here. You probably have an entire file Detective Davis gave you. Do you see cops, too? Or just criminals?"

"Both," she answers flatly.

I nod slowly.

"Is that important to you?"

"Do you see Jax?"

"Who?"

"Detective Davis."

"Doctor-patient confidentiality."

"Right." I rest my elbows on my knees. "I'll take that as a yes."

She sighs. "So you have problems controlling your temper?"

"You got all that from the two minutes I've been here or from my file?"

"This will go a lot easier if you actually answer my questions. That's how this works. I ask, you answer. We find your issues and we work through them together."

I roll my eyes. "You're saying I have issues? You don't even know me."

"You're here, right?"

I avert my gaze and look at the frames on the walls again.

She adds, "Can you tell me why you're so angry?"

My gaze trails back to her, and I mumble, "Again, shouldn't that be your job?"

Her eyes move slowly from mine down to the notepad on her lap as she jots down God knows what. After a minute of listening to the pen scrape against the paper, she places both of them on the couch next to her. Then she crosses her arms and says, "My first crush was Taylor Hanson. You know that boy band Hanson? You might be a little young. Anyway, the middle one. When I first saw their music video, I thought he was a girl and didn't think twice about them. When I found out he was a boy, I started to pay attention. Of course, crushing on a guy you thought was a girl can do bad things to a pre-teen's sexual assumption. It's safe to say I questioned my sexuality for a good year after. I tried to like the older brother; he was more manly, but I kept going back to Taylor—"

"What the hell are you talking about?" I cut in.

She shrugs. "I'm paid by the hour. *You* need to be here. If you won't talk, *I* will."

My eyes narrow, all words lost somewhere between us.

Dr. Aroma continues, "So the older Hanson brother didn't really—"

"Jesus Christ. Okay! Ask your damn questions."

Smirking, she straightens up and puts the professional mask back in place. "So, Ky, why do you think you have anger issues?"

"I don't," I say, point-blank.

"Your file says different."

"I was having a bad day."

"Oh yeah?"

"Yeah."

"Tell me about it."

I suck in a breath and release it with a huff. Then I give in to the inevitable, because maybe she's right. Maybe it'll be easier this way. "I'd just left a buddy's funeral."

Dr. Aroma quirks an eyebrow. "And how did that make you feel?"

I scratch the back of my head in irritation. "How do *you* think it made me feel?"

"*Angry*, I suppose, considering the outcome."

"I didn't do it because I was angry. I did it because if I didn't, one of my brothers would have. They have wives, kids, *lives.* They have a lot more to lose than I do."

"And why do you think you have nothing to lose?"

My irritation turns up a notch. I've avoided thinking about it since that day, and I'll continue to avoid it. "If I give you all of this now, we'll have nothing left to talk about."

"I'm sure we can find other things," she says, picking up her notepad and pen again.

"So this Taylor Hanson..."

She fakes a smile but goes along with my need to change the subject. I let her yammer on about her celebrity crushes during her teen years. The entire time, I fail at not thinking about Garcia, his parents, and his pregnant wife, who cried through the entire funeral. It should have been me.

"Ky?" she asks, pulling me from my thoughts.

"Huh?"

"Do you have anyone in your life you can talk to?"

"Again, isn't that what you're here for?"

She smiles, but it's tight. "That's a shame. Maybe you should work on that. I'm positive it will help... a lot more than you listening to me talk about the kid who played The Real Boy in *Casper.*" She slaps her knees and stands up. "Today was good. You did well. Take my advice, Ky, and I'll see you next time."

* * *

Ky: *On a scale of one to ten, how mandatory is this therapy bullshit?*
Jackson: *Eleven.*

* * *

STEPPING OFF THE elevator and onto my floor, the sight before me makes me forget everything. I've wanted to bump into Madison since the first time I saw her. Hell, I'd take ogling her from afar. I even stood in front of her door a few times and raised my hand to knock. At the last second, I stopped myself and questioned what the hell I was doing. My game was rusty at best. The times I'd been home from tour, I was always with my buddies. We'd wear our uniforms, walk into a place, and the deal was practically sealed. Now I was alone, and Madison doesn't seem like the type to give a shit about my uniform—though I'd be lying if I said the thought hadn't crossed my mind.

She sits with her back to her door, her knees up and her arms covering her head. "Hey..." I say cautiously, standing in front of her.

She looks up, her eyes glazed and her cheeks wet.

I squat down so we're eye to eye. "You okay?"

She shakes her head.

"What's going on?"

She speaks so quietly I almost don't hear her. "I locked myself out."

"Is the maintenance guy out?"

"The what?" she asks, and I can't help but laugh.

"How long have you been sitting here?"

She shrugs. "An hour. Not sure."

"And this is why you're crying?"

She frowns and wipes her tears. "I didn't know there was a maintenance guy." Standing up, she brushes her hands down her shirt. "And please don't laugh at me." She crosses her arms, keeping her eyes cast downward. "I already feel stupid enough."

I stand up, too. "I'm sorry. I didn't mean to make you—"

"Where is he?"

"Who?"

"The guy who's going to let me back into my apartment."

I pull out my phone and dial the number I was given when I moved in a month ago. I give him the apartment number, and he shows up a minute later with a master key. "Enjoy," he says, winking at us.

Her eyebrows pinch as she watches him walk away.

"Madison." It feels good to be able to say her name—to *her*—*out loud*, instead of just in my head, over and over. "I'm sorry if I made you feel stupid, I—"

Her forced smile cuts me off. "It's fine, Ky. Good night." She steps into her apartment and quickly shuts the door.

I look at the time.

It's one in the afternoon.

8

Madison: *I locked myself out today.*

Sara: *Did you call the maintenance guy?*

Madison: *I didn't know to do that.*

Sara: *So how did you get in?*

Madison: *Ky.*

Sara: *?*

Madison: *He called the guy.*

Sara: *Did you let him into your apartment?*

Madison: *No. He just unlocked the door and left.*

Sara: *I meant Ky.*

Madison: *No. Should I have?*

Sara: *I have no idea.*

Madison: *I hate this.*

Sara: *Me too.*

9

KY

"Hı," Madison squeaks, looking down at the pizza box in my hand.

"Your place or mine?" I try to joke, but the shakiness in my voice betrays the confidence I'm trying to exude. She doesn't move. I square my shoulders and clear my throat. She still doesn't respond. After a beat, I tell her, "It's my form of an apology."

"For what?" she asks, brow bunched in genuine confusion.

"For earlier... when you were locked out and I laughed at you."

"I'm sorry. I was just super sensitive after the shitty day I'd had." She opens the door fully and steps to the side. I don't hesitate. Not for a second. "I like pizza," she says, following behind me as I walk to her kitchen. Her apartment's the same layout as mine, only opposite. The front door opens to the living room, kitchen to the right, two bedrooms on the left, and a bathroom and laundry room between them. "How much do I owe you?" she asks.

I wave her off. "Nothing, it's a gift... for both of us, really."

"A gift for you, too?"

I turn to her and swallow my nerves—Dr. Aroma's advice replaying in my head. "Well, you kind of have to eat it with me."

She smiles, a shy kind of smile that completely intrigues me. "I can do that."

MADISON

I THINK I'M doing a good job of hiding my nerves. It's not just his presence that makes me nervous. It's everything. "When did you move in?" he asks.

I finish chewing my pizza. "The day you found me fighting a war with your mailbox."

He laughs. *I made him laugh.* "Are you from around here, Madison?"

I stand and pick up my plate and the now empty box of pizza off the coffee table and set them down on the kitchen counter. Then I try to focus on exactly what it is my answer should be. "Yes," I tell him and hope it's enough.

"Oh yeah? Whereabouts?"

I tense for a moment, my eyes shut tight, trying desperately not to panic. "Just around." I turn to him, but he's right there, inches in front of me. His eyes narrow as he searches mine. "Madison," he says through an exhale.

My breath catches.

He smiles. "You wanna watch TV or something?"

"You don't wanna go home?"

"Are you kicking me out?"

I shrug again. "Just don't want to take up all of your time."

"I can't imagine a better way to spend my time."

I drop my gaze to the floor, my cheeks warming with my blush.

"So?"

I stare at his feet. And then I inhale sharply and muster the courage to look up at him. "Your place or mine?"

He smiles.

Stupid dimples.

* * *

THE LIGHTS ARE off. A show about renovating houses is on. We're sitting on my couch, and his leg is touching my leg. I want to move away, but there's no room. He clears his throat and leans forward, causing his leg to press harder against mine. "So," I start and then stop myself when I realize how loud I was. I inhale a calming breath before continuing. "Do you work? I mean, I'm sure you work, but what do you do? For work?" It might be possible that I've somehow lost the ability to form complete, proper sentences.

"I'm between jobs," he says, leaning back and throwing his arm behind me. "You?"

I can feel his eyes burning on me. "Kind of the same."

"I thought maybe you'd be in college or something."

"No," I say, staring ahead. *He's been thinking about me?*

"How old are you?"

I turn to him, eyebrows pinched. "How old are *you?*"

"Twenty-three."

"Twenty-two."

He nods, his eyes fixed on mine. "Nice."

"Nice?"

His phone sounds, and he sighs, reaches into his pocket. Biting his lip, he reads the message before looking up at me. "It's been real nice, Madison. We should do this again some-time." He's already on his feet before he finishes speaking.

I walk him to the door, and once he's in the hallway, he turns and looks at me. I wait for him to say something. When nothing comes but an empty stare, I panic and shut the door in his face.

KY

"WHAT TOOK YOU so long?" Jackson asks when he answers the phone.

"Sorry. I was preoccupied."

"Ky," he says impatiently.

"I was just talking to my neighbor."

"A girl?"

"So what if it was?"

"You can't be distracted."

"Are you serious right now?"

"I can't have this shit fuck up... not over some girl. You need to be focused. In control. All the time." After a pause, he adds, "You know what this assignment means to me."

"Maybe you've forgotten that Steven was *my* brother." I rub my palm across my jaw and throw myself on the couch, trying to tone down my anger. "I get it, Jax. I know that this is important. It's important to both of us. I know what this means, and that's why I'd never do anything to jeopardize that. You have to trust me, just like I trust you. She's just a girl. She doesn't mean anything."

"Good," he says. "Is she hot?"

I laugh. "It's ridiculous how hot she is."

"Hotter than Ashlee?"

All air leaves my lungs. "She's better."

KY: AGE SIXTEEN

"*I JUST DON'T understand why he has to follow us everywhere,*" *Ashlee said.*

I glanced over at Jackson sitting on the couch in the living room, on the Xbox with a couple of guys, while the party went on around him. "He's not bothering anyone. He just wants to hang out. What's the big deal?"

Her hands flattened against my chest as she kicked off the wall. She rose to her toes, her breath fanning my ear when she said, "I just want some alone time with you. We've been together six months, and he's always around. What happens if I ask you to take me upstairs to fool around? Is he going to come knocking on every door looking for you?"

I pulled back so I could see her face. She was buzzed but not so out of it that she didn't know what she was saying. I raised my eyebrows in question. She bit her lip and nodded. And that was all I needed. I grabbed her hand and led her to the back of the couch, where I leaned over and told Jackson exactly where I'd be and what I'd be doing. He nodded, his eyes never leaving the TV. Then I led her upstairs to an empty room. She slipped out of her dress and stood there in nothing but her underwear and heels. Goddamn, she was sexy. She was the hottest girl in the entire school. Somehow, luck was on my side and she chose me. "Lock the door," she said.

I obliged.

She lay back on the bed, one of her hands going between her legs. "Come here."

I obliged again.

After five minutes of making out and grinding and hands and fingers anywhere and everywhere, she finally said, "Make love to me, Ky."

I, of course, obliged.

* * *

I SPENT EVERY spare second over the next few months with Ashlee. We'd find ways to sneak around just to have sex. By then, Christine had turned her craft room into my room, so I had my own space. I'd sneak her in while everyone was asleep. Jackson knew, but he'd never rat me out.

The day I turned seventeen, the family took me out to dinner. It was low-key, the way I wanted it. I'd invited Steve, my brother, to join us, but he said he had to work and he'd pick me up after to do something, just the two of us.

Steve, nineteen at the time, had dropped out of school a while ago. He surfed from one couch to another until his friends finally kicked him out.

A few weeks after I'd moved in, Christine invited him over for dinner. To say it was awkward was an understatement. Christine fussed about the entire event, making sure Steven felt comfortable. I could tell he tried, but it was hard for him. He'd grown up the way I did, so he wasn't used to the attention. At one point, he pulled out his wallet and emptied the content on the table. "It's not much," he said, "but it should cover Ky's meals and board for a few weeks. I'll get more to you later."

Christine told him to hush. Jeff told him it wasn't necessary. I looked on in shock, not knowing what to do. It was more than just an offering from Steve's end though, and I understood where he was coming from. Especially when I sat with him out on the porch after dinner while he had a smoke. His eyes were fixed on our old house. I say house because it was never a home. Not like it was with the Davises. "I'm sorry, Ky," he said. "I should've been there."

"You didn't know," I told him. "You couldn't have changed it."

He shook his head. "Not just that night. I mean all the nights before that." He rubbed his eyes, and for the first time in my life, I saw my brother as more than just my brother. I saw him as a man. And as a kid. All at once. "I should've taken you with me when I left. I just wanted to get out of there so bad that I didn't—" he broke off with a sigh. Steve—he was a good guy—at least to me. To the outside world, however, he was sketchy at best. He spent his time between flipping burgers at a ratty diner downtown and partying hard. By 'partying hard', I meant copious amounts of drugs and alcohol. And even *though I was around it my entire life, he still managed to keep that part of himself hidden from me—and I was grateful for that.*

I didn't need to watch his decline on top of everything else. "I was so selfish, Ky. And I hate myself for letting this shit happen to you." He looked up at me and then into the house behind us where we could hear Christine's unrestricted laugh. "I'm just glad it worked out for you. It's not too late to turn your life around. You don't have to become a statistic, Ky. You can be anything you want now."

AFTER HOURS OF *waiting for Steve at home, and numerous unreturned phone calls, I pushed aside the disappointment and anger and called Ashlee. I needed a release. I knew she was always up for that. "Is Steve here?" Christine asked as I passed the living room. Jackson didn't look up from the TV. I knew he was upset, though he'd never admit it. He wanted to go out for my birthday, even if Steve was involved. Jax saw Steve like the rest of the world did—a nomad with no ambition and no future. But Steve loved me and I loved him. We were blood brothers and nothing could take that away, even him standing me up on my birthday.*

I shook my head and switched focus from Jackson to Christine. "No. I can't get ahold of him," I said. "I'm just going to Ashlee's for a bit—if that's okay?"

"Sure, sweetheart. Have fun." Christine smiled, then rolled her eyes when Jackson scoffed.

"What? You want to hang out at Ashlee's? You're more than welcome," I offered.

His eyes snapped to mine—his jaw hanging open.

I sighed. "Seriously. You can tag along."

His face fell. "I'm good, Ky." He turned back to the TV, but his eyes were cast downward. "Happy birthday," he muttered.

Jeff cleared his throat. "We can do something, son," he said, speaking to Jackson. His gaze flicked to me quickly, and even though it was a split second, I could see the disappointment. Hell, I could feel the disappointment in the entire room. Jeff added, "How 'bout you show me that aura game on the Zbox?"

Jackson chuckled. Shit, he was such a kid. "Halo, Dad. And Xbox."

Christine stood up. "I'll make some cookies," she stated, rubbing my arm as she passed me. She lowered her voice, her words meant only for me. "Have a good time, Ky. Be safe."

I watched Christine make her way to the kitchen, and Jackson and Jeff move to the Xbox set up under the TV. Jax started to explain what everything was while Jeff listened intently.

At that moment, there was a part of me that didn't want to leave —but it would just be out of pity for Jax and he'd know it. He'd hate it, too. So, I stepped out of the house with a smug smile, my body already anticipating the night ahead with Ashlee.

A SHLEE'S PARENTS WERE away for the weekend. She left the front door unlocked and was already naked in her bed waiting for me.

We fucked twice before she told me she was hungry.

I took her to the ratty diner downtown, hoping to find Steve busy and forced to work late so he'd at least have an excuse as to why he stood me up.

He was there, just not working.

"This place is disgusting, Ky," Ashlee whined, her hand gripping my arm extra tight.

I ignored her and marched up to Steve, who was sitting in a booth with a bunch of other people, his arms around girls on either side of him.

Conversation stopped when I stepped up next to their table, and he was the first to look up, his eyes bloodshot, his lids heavy. Most likely from whatever the fuck he'd been taking. "Baby bro!" He smiled and threw his hand out for me.

I smacked it away.

Two dudes in the booth stood up.

Steve raised his hand to stop them from going any further.

"We need to get out of here," Ashlee said.

I ignored her again.

"You know I waited for you for hours."

"What are you talking about?"

I couldn't contain my anger anymore. "You, you asshole! You were supposed to pick me up after the family birthday dinner."

His face fell. Then he pushed one of the girls out of the booth and stood toe-to-toe with me. "You know they're not actually your family, right?"

I shoved his chest. "And what? You are? Where the fuck have you been the last couple of years? You've come around, what? Four times? That's not fucking enough, Steve!" I scoffed and looked down on him. "Don't stand there and tell me they're not my family. They're here—where the fuck are you?"

"Fuck you, Kyler," he growled, shoving me back.

"No, Steve. Fuck you!"

Ashlee squealed.

Steve's friends got out of the booth.

I waved my finger in Steve's face. "You getting fucking high is more important than your own brother? Nice. Real fucking nice! That's exactly the shit I had to put up with with Mom and Dad. I thought you were different, but you're just as pathetic and fucked up as they are!"

He got the first punch in.

I got the next three.

We were told to leave.

We did.

"YOU'RE SUCH A *fucking Neanderthal, Ky,"* Ashlee said once we were back in the car. I turned to her, but she was smirking. "It's kind of hot." We skipped the food and went back to her place, where we repeated the events from earlier that night. Halfway through the second round, my phone rang. It was Christine. I ignored it.

Two minutes later, it rang again. This time, it was Jax.

I looked at the time. It was past midnight—past curfew. I

switched it to silent. I didn't want to deal with it. I wanted to forget this shitty night. And Ashlee—she was helping me do that.

WE FELL ASLEEP in each other's arms and didn't wake till morning. The panic I felt when I initially woke was nothing compared to how I felt when I looked at my phone. Over a hundred missed calls—all from Christine and Jax. The panic increased tenfold when I called Christine to apologize. Her voice was a shaky whisper. "You need to come home, Ky. Right now. It's Jeff."

WHEN I GOT home, Christine was sitting on the couch, Jackson next to her, holding her hand.

She didn't even look up when I called out to her. "He's gone, Ky. Jeff... he's gone."

Jackson wrapped her in his arms.

He, too, refused to look at me.

WHILE I WAS too busy thinking with my dick the night before, Jeff and Jax had set up the Xbox. They'd been playing for a while when one of the controllers died. Jeff went to the store, no more than five minutes away, to buy new batteries.

He got the batteries, but he never made it home.

He was T-boned at an intersection by a drunk driver who'd run a red light.

THEY BARELY SPOKE to me in the three days leading up to the funeral. I saw them leaving once and asked where they were going. Jackson answered, said they were picking out the casket.

They didn't ask me to join them.

I wasn't even mad.

ASHLEE, BEING THE perfect girlfriend, sat next to me and held my hand the entire funeral. Christine sat on my other side, holding my other hand, and Jackson sat next to her with his arm around her.

ASHLEE WENT HOME after the funeral to watch her little sister, and I felt like a stranger in the only place I'd ever felt was home.

Christine and Jackson cried. A lot.

I tried to force myself to cry, but I couldn't.

I carried too much guilt to mourn.

It should've been me in that car.

If I'd stayed home and hung out with Jackson like I should've, it wouldn't have happened—at least not to Jeff.

Jeff—he was the greatest man I'd ever known. What other kind of man willingly saves a kid—allows him into his home without question? He went out of his way to make sure I was part of his family. And what the hell did I do to repay him? Nothing.

Not a goddamn thing.

After an hour of being invisible, I left and drove to Ashlee's house.

It was then I realized Ashlee wasn't the perfect girlfriend—that was made evident by the moans she emitted while some guy fucked her in the same bed we were in the exact moment Jeff died.

She screamed when she saw me.

The guy jumped up, naked as the day he was born.

I didn't know him.

And I didn't care to.

But my fist did. It went through eight blows to his face of caring.

Ashlee cried and called after me.

I got in my car and drove back to the cemetery, where I kicked the fresh dirt lying on top of Jeff's body.

Then I fell to my knees.

And it finally happened.

I broke.

And I cried seventeen years' worth of tears.

And it didn't fucking help.

Not even a little bit.

Not even at all.

10

KY

DR. AROMA TAPS her pen on a notepad a few times while she openly glares at me and I glare back. I've been in her office a good ten minutes, and neither of us has spoken a word. I don't know what game she's playing—but I can go with this shit all day long. She's the first to crack, breaking the silence with a sigh. "So are you ready for the list of boys I slept with during college?"

"Is this how you get all your clients to talk to you?"

She nods, her smile full force. "It works."

Leaning back in my chair, I rest my ankle on the opposite knee and wave a hand in the air. "Ask your questions, Doc."

"Nah." She shrugs. "I think I'm just going to let you talk this session."

"I think I'd rather sit in silence."

"Okay then," she says, her eyes never leaving mine.

And so the game begins again.

Only this time, she doesn't stare; she scribbles in her stupid notepad instead. I sit up higher, curious as to what the hell she could be writing, and this goes on for ten minutes. Occasionally she'll eye the ceiling as if deep in thought before continuing to write, and my curiosity wins out. "What the hell notes could you possibly be obtaining from me sitting here?"

She shakes her head. "These aren't notes about you. It's a list of my college conquests." She glances up at me. "You wanna see?"

"No."

"Want to talk then?"

"No."

Pressing her lips together, she looks back down at the page. "Colin. Freshman year. He was so dreamy. Wait. I *think* his name's Colin. Could be Chris. Or Craig. Either way—"

"So I met a girl," I blurt out. I don't know if it's because I want her to shut up or because I haven't stopped thinking about Madison.

Dr. Aroma's smile is instant. "Oh yeah?"

I clear my throat. "Yeah."

"And how did that make you feel?"

"Really?"

She releases the tiniest of laughs. "No. Not really. Tell me about her, though," she says, setting the pen and paper down to give me her full attention.

"There's not much to say, honestly. She's my neighbor. We had pizza. Then I guess I maybe tried to kiss her."

"And how did that go?"

"She squealed and slammed the door in my face."

Doc laughs again. "And how did that make you feel?"

Excited, I want to say. But instead, I play it down and shrug.

Her smile gets wider, as if she knows my real answer. "And have you wanted to punch anything since said door-slamming incident, Kyler?"

"Nope."

* * *

DeLuca: *Meet me at O'Malley's bar at 1600, soldier.*
Ky: *I'll be there.*

* * *

I CALL JACKSON from my department-issued phone as soon as I get the text on my walk home from therapy. "DeLuca contacted me. I'm meeting him this afternoon."

"Nothing's registered on your phone."

"Yeah, you're going to have to somehow transfer my real number to this one. I don't want to give him a new number."

"Shit. I should've thought of that."

"Hey, you're the detective."

"Smartass."

"Love you, too."

* * *

MADISON'S THE FIRST thing I see when I step off the elevator on my way to meet DeLuca. Again, she's standing in front of the mailboxes, peering inside hers. "You must really like mail," I call out.

She spins around, laughing when she sees me. "I think it's more the element of surprise that I'm drawn to."

"Surprise?"

"Yeah. It's more the not knowing if something's going to be there and then one day... *surprise!*" she sings, moving toward me.

With a chuckle, I open the door for us and step out into the fresh air. She squints, trying to block out the sun as she looks up at me.

"Funny," I tell her, trying to hide my smile. "The only things I get are bills and credit card applications."

"I can't wait," she says, grinning from ear-to-ear. "You want to go for a walk or something?"

"I can't," I tell her honestly. "I have to meet someone."

Her smile drops. "Well, are you walking, because maybe I could walk with you?"

"It's kind of personal."

"Oh." Swear it—she looks as disappointed as I feel. "A girl?"

"No," I say, pushing down the excitement at her reaction. "Not a girl. Promise."

* * *

DeLuca's already at O'Malley's, sitting at the bar, beer in one hand and phone in the other.

I pass Tiny, who's sitting at the opposite end, and silently take the seat next to DeLuca.

He looks up, startled, and then quickly drops the phone on the bar—face down. He chugs the rest of his beer, then nods toward a door a few feet away. "Let's go." Not surprisingly, he leads me down to the basement. "What do you think?" he asks.

"About what?"

"The venue?"

"What the fuck are you talking about?"

His eyes widen slightly, as if surprised by my tone. If he's waiting for me to apologize, he'll be waiting a long-ass time. "Your debut fight. Here. One month. One of my fighters got injured. You think you're up for it?"

"I don't care where I fight. I just want to fight."

"Good." He starts to climb back up the stairs. "Keep your phone on you at all times." He stops at the top step and turns to me. "You want to fight? You do what I say, when I say it. You're in my world now, *soldier*."

On the outside, I force myself to nod. Inside, there's an anger brewing deep and low in my gut. I know people like him—the kind to think their time and their words hold more value than everyone else's. I hate people like him. Hell, I was raised by people like him.

He returns my nod and leaves through the same door we came in from.

I stand in the middle of the basement, waiting to see if he's coming back. When enough time has passed and I assume he's left, I walk around the room. The only other door leads to a hallway. At the end of the hall are two doors, opposite each other. I make my way over and open the one on my left. The room's empty, just like the one on my right. I pull out my phone—"What the fuck are you doing?" DeLuca snaps. He stands in the doorway with his arms crossed over his faded gray shirt, his biceps flexing against the sleeves. His head tilts to the side, his eyes narrowed, waiting for me to answer. "So?" he pushes.

He's trying to be intimidating.

It *almost* works.

I match his stance. "Just checking things out."

We stand, eyes locked, waiting for the other to break first.

He visibly swallows.

I raise my chin.

"Right," he finally says, his gaze shifting to the basement stairs. He starts to back away and slowly shakes his head at someone who must be waiting at the top of the stairs, but the movement's so slight I almost don't notice.

But I do. Just like I notice the nine-millimeter hidden in his waistband.

* * *

AFTER SNAPPING A few pictures on my phone, I send them to Jackson. He calls when I'm a block away from my building. "I have no idea what you just sent me," he says.

I check behind me to make sure I'm not being followed. I fucked up—dropped the ball—and DeLuca has every right to start being suspicious. Ducking my head and keeping my voice low, I tell him, "It's the basement of O'Malley's. That's where I'll be fighting in a month... Dude," I lower my voice again. "DeLuca's packing heat. Should I be surprised?"

"Are you surprised or are you worried? Because if you're worried, let me know right now and I'll end this."

"Don't be dramatic. I was just asking."

He sighs. "I don't know, man. The guy's a complete mystery, wrapped in an enigma, covered in suspicion. We tail him for days and *nothing*. He's home, at a bar, or at the gym. Nothing else. What he does and who he meets? No one knows." He pauses for a moment. "The guy has to be wicked smart to cover all his tracks. It just doesn't make sense."

I shake my head and push open the door to my building. "You know I'm in this, Jax, but maybe we need to sit down and discuss what I should be..." My words die in the air when I see Madison—or at least the back of her. She's changed into tiny denim cutoffs and a tight tank. I wouldn't have recognized her if not for the fact that she was searching through her damn mailbox again.

"Ky?" Jax says.

"Hang on," I tell him, then cover the phone with my hand. I raise my voice so Madison can hear me. "I'm getting a little jealous of all the attention that mailbox is getting from you."

Her head throws back with her laugh. "Ky, Ky, Ky," she says, turning to me.

"Holy shit," I say quietly, but going by the smirk on her face, I wasn't quiet enough.

She has curves upon curves.

Endless legs.

Phenomenal tits.

I wonder what they'd feel like in my hands. On my face. In my mouth. "Ky!" Jax yells.

I hold the phone to my ear, my eyes never leaving her ridiculous body. "I'll call you back." I hang up and return Madison's smirk. "How 'bout that walk now?"

She purses her lips and eyes the ceiling. "Well, Ky, there's absolutely nothing more in this entire world I'd love to do than go for a walk with you..." Her eyes shift back to me before shrugging. Then she fakes a grimace and inhales loudly. "But unfortunately I have somewhere to be, and I can't get out of it."

"Liar."

She shrugs again. "It's true." She steps around me and heads for the door. "But it's always a pleasure running into you. We should do it more often. Maybe next time I'll supply the pizza."

MADISON

I LIED. I had nowhere to go. But the way his eyes widened when he saw me and the way he was looking at me... I couldn't be around him a second longer. My heart was pounding way too hard, way too fast.

I was told to flirt with him, to dress in a way that would get his attention and make him want to spend time with me. It worked. Now if only *I* could work around him, everything would be fine.

The moment I'm out the doors, a panic sets in. I don't know where to go. I go left and hope that the decision is fast enough that he doesn't find it suspicious.

I walk half a block until I see a tiny little café. There's no one sitting on the tables outside, and I pray that it's the same inside. It's not that I don't like people. It's just that I'm not used to them. Luckily, there's only one person in there, and he's too preoccupied on his computer to notice my existence. "Hi. I'll have a coffee," I tell the bored-looking guy behind the counter.

He rolls his eyes and sighs heavily, inspecting his nails. "Americano, Latte, Misto, Mocha, Cappuccino, Macchiato or Espresso?"

I gulp nervously and take a step back. I have no idea what he just said. "Just coffee that tastes like coffee," I squeak.

Dean, I've worked out from his name badge, quirks an eyebrow and slowly points to the corner of the store where a table's set up with what I assume is a thermal coffee dispenser.

I try to smile at him. "Thanks," I say, reaching into my pocket. "What do I owe you?"

He leans on his elbows and eyes me curiously. And then he scoffs. Right in my damn face. "That coffee tastes like burnt asshole. I'd pay *you* to drink it."

"Nice. I'll think of that when I'm sipping on it." I sit on the opposite end of the room from computer guy and drink my burnt-asshole flavored coffee, which doesn't actually taste like burnt asshole. It tastes like every other coffee I remember having.

Four cups later and I can no longer ignore my need to pee. I look around but there doesn't seem to be a bathroom here, so I leave quietly and make my way back to the apartment—*my* apartment. I wait impatiently for the elevator and practically jump in when the doors open. I squeeze my legs together and do everything possible to avoid having to cup my privates. When the elevator doors open on my floor, I run to my apartment, rifling through the contents of my bag for my keys. "Fuck!"

"Madison?" Ky's standing in his doorway now, arms at his side. "I was thinking—"

"Pee!"

"What?"

I push past him and run into his apartment. "I need to pee!"

KY

MADISON DROPS HER purse on the couch as soon as she enters my apartment and runs to the bathroom.

She's laughing.

She's on the toilet *laughing*.

And peeing.

I don't even know how I'm supposed to feel right now. "Madison?"

"Don't talk to me while I'm peeing!"

"Okay..." I say through a chuckle and look down at the contents of her purse, now spilled out onto the cushion. Quickly, I scan her stuff: mace, a pocketknife, a kubaton, and a rape whistle.

Girl's prepared.

She starts laughing harder.

"Are you good?" I shout.

"I had to go so bad!" She opens the door and says, "Why is it that your bladder always seems to try to tip you over the edge just as you're at your door? It's strange, right?"

"I think maybe you're strange, Madison," I joke.

She freezes in her spot when she sees me standing over her stuff. Clearing her throat, she walks over and starts placing the items in her bag.

"That's a lot of protection you're carrying," I tell her.

She ignores my remark and sits down on the couch,

holding her bag on her lap. "For someone who doesn't work, you're not home often."

I sit next to her. "You noticed?"

"What do you do?" she asks, ignoring me again.

I sigh, now realizing what it must be like for good old Cinnamon Aroma to have to deal with my evasiveness. "Not much. Gym and errands." I grab the remote and turn on the TV, hoping to put an end to her questioning.

"What kind of errands?"

What am I supposed to say? Court ordered therapy? Undercover drug bust? I change the subject. "Where did you go anyway?"

She faces me, folding her leg beneath her. "Just to this coffee place a block away."

"You meet up with a friend?"

"No. Just by myself."

"But you said that you *had* to be somewhere and couldn't get out of it."

Her face falls, her smile completely wiped now. "I just..."

"Just...?"

"Um..." She starts to stand up, but I grab her arm to stop her from moving.

Her gaze moves to the door, like she's searching for a polite way to bail. I don't want her to leave, so I say, "I'm bored. You want to get out of here?"

Her eyes widen. "What?"

"Yeah." I stand up. "Let's do something."

"Like what?" she asks, her brow bunched.

"I don't know. What do you want to do?"

Her gaze drops to her lap. "Do you..." she trails off.

"Do I what?"

"I've always wanted to go to dinner and a movie."

"Like a date?"

She gasps quietly. "No. Not a date. Just—I don't know.

Maybe?" Her eyes flick to mine, the uncertainty in them clear.

"Wait. You've never gone to dinner and a movie?"

She shakes her head slowly—her eyes fixed on mine. "No."

"So what do you do on dates?"

"I've never dated," she says slowly, each word more unsure than the last.

I just stare, too dumbstruck to speak.

"Can we go now?" she asks, her words rushed. "Never mind. I'll just go home." She stands quickly.

I grab her hand. "Are you ready to go?"

Her smile is all-consuming. "Let me change real quick."

MADISON

Madison: So he asked me out.

Sara: Yeah? Are you going?

Madison: Yes… we're going to dinner and a movie.

I rush around the room, changing clothes and shoes, and putting on what little make-up I wear. My phone never leaves my hand. I squeeze it so tight my knuckles turn white.

The phone is my lifeline. My security blanket. It's my past and my future. And it's my only connection to the one person who truly knows me.

I sit on the edge of the bed and stare at the screen, waiting anxiously for a reply. The feeling of dread over-shadows my excitement. Just as the tears start pooling in my eyes and I can no longer feel my heart's beat over its slow, torturous *break*, the phone sounds with a text.

Sara: Good.

A knock on the door interrupts my reply, or at least my thoughts of *how* to reply. I have nothing. No words of comfort. Nothing.

"Maddy!" Ky yells, just as I stand. "Are you there?"

By the time I get to the door, I can hear him laughing on the other side. "Yeah?" I yell back.

His laugh gets louder. "I don't know how long I should have waited before picking you up. What's the normal protocol on how long it takes a girl to get ready? Should I leave and come back? Or even better—you can let me in and change in front of me!"

My mouth drops open. It's still like that when I open the door to his sexy-as-sin smirk. I grab his arm and roughly pull him into the apartment. "Everyone can hear you!"

He chuckles, then stops abruptly as he crosses his arms and scans me from head to toe. He gets to my bare feet and licks his lips. "I have a thing for short skirts and bare feet," he mumbles. "You better cover them, or we're gonna skip the date and stay in."

I try to inhale, but the air is too thick and I squeak, "You said you'd take me to dinner and a movie."

He nods slowly, his eyes moving back up to my face, slowing for a split-second on my breasts. "Let's go then."

KY

I ASK HER if she wants to go anywhere in particular. She says she isn't sure—that she doesn't know the area that well. Odd, considering she'd told me earlier that she's from around here.

We walk a few blocks to a hole in the wall Italian joint. She doesn't drive, and I don't have a car.

"Is Ky short for anything?" Madison asks just as the waiter comes by and lazily drops our plates on the table.

"Kyler," I tell her.

She smiles and repeats it a few times. I've always hated the name, but hearing it fall from her lips has me second-guessing my feelings.

"Does it have a meaning?"

"It's Danish for a bowman."

"A bowman?" she asks, the confusion clear in her voice.

"Yeah, like an archer."

She scrunches her nose and tilts her head to the side. "An archer? What the hell is an archer?"

"A strong, masculine dude who uses a bow and arrow."

"Ohh!" She almost yells. "An *archer*," she repeats as if the word suddenly has new meaning. "Why didn't you just say that?"

"I did!"

"Kyler," she muses. "I like it." She leans forward. "You don't?"

I shake my head. "I got called Kylie too much as a kid and—"

Her burst of laughter interrupts me. I raise an eyebrow, which just makes her laugh harder. "So anyway..." I say loud enough to drown her out. "I go by Ky and you are never, *ever* to call me Kyler."

She stops laughing, her expression completely serious now. "You got it, *Kyler*."

"Smartass." I cross my arms and watch her try to keep her shit together. "I regret telling you now."

"No, you don't," she says, sitting up higher. "Life's too short for regrets."

"What about you?" I ask. "What does Madison mean?"

She shrugs. "Have you got any brothers or sisters?"

I fake a smile. "Another time maybe?"

She looks disappointed but says, "Sure."

"Besides, I need to keep you intrigued, right? How else am I going to keep you around?"

Her gaze lowers. "You don't need to worry. I'm already intrigued."

JUST LIKE WITH dinner, she asks I choose a movie for us. She says she doesn't care. It's not about the movie; it's the experience. As a joke, I ask her if she's ever been to a movie before. She shrugs and changes the subject.

"YOU WANT TO make out?" I whisper in her ear.

It's meant as a joke, but she clearly doesn't get it because she slowly turns from the screen to me, eyes wide. "What?"

I try to get her to relax a little. "You said you wanted the experience, right? Hot date... dark theater... it's all about the making out."

Her brow bunches, her eyes darting everywhere as a million thoughts run through her pretty little head.

A chuckle filters out of me. "I was just messing around, Maddy."

She squirms in her seat. "So you *don't* want to kiss me?"

"Oh, I do... trust me." I fake a yawn and stretch my arms in the air, then settle one around her shoulders. "But I can wait."

She looks back at me with a hint of a smile.

"Hey... the fake-yawn, arm-around-your-girl move is the best part of the movie experience."

She smiles full force now, not looking away.

I grip her shoulder and point to the screen with my free hand. "The movie's that way."

"You called me your girl."

I grimace. "I haven't dated since I was seventeen, so I may be a little rusty."

Her eyes practically bug out of her head.

"Watch the movie, Madison," I tell her, just as my phone vibrates in my pocket.

Jackson: We need to talk.
Ky: I'm out.

Jackson calls, but I reject it.

Ky: Can't talk. I'm at the movies.
Jackson: This is serious, Ky. I'm not fucking around.

"I've got to go to the bathroom," I whisper to Madison.

She nods, her focus on the movie.

Once I'm out in the foyer, I call Jackson. "Hey," he answers.

"What's up?"

"Are you on a date?"

"Kind of."

"Neighbor girl?"

"You said this was urgent."

"I don't want you to worry," he rushes out.

"But?"

"DeLuca was seen leaving your apartment building today. No one saw him go in, just out."

I release a frustrated breath. "So he knows where I live?"

"Yeah…" He pauses a beat. "I don't want to be a dick, but you're starting to date this girl—"

"I'm not dating her," I cut in. "We're on a could-be date. There's a difference."

"Whatever. The fact is she's already a distraction. You keep it going with her and she becomes part of the mess. You want her in that danger?"

"There's nothing going on, and even if there was, I can keep the two separated."

"No, Ky, you can't. When you fall for a girl, you fall hard. She infiltrates every part of you… she *becomes* you. You remember Ashlee, right?"

And with that, I hang up.

MADISON

I WAITED UNTIL I knew he was no longer in the theater before pulling out my phone and sending a message.

Madison: *I think he wants to kiss me.*

Sara: *You think?*
Madison: *No. I know. He asked.*
Sara: *Well at least he asked…*
Madison: *You have to tell me what to do.*
Madison: *…*
Madison: *…*

I don't get a response until Ky walks in a few minutes later.

Sara: *Do it.*
Sara: *Don't let him touch you.*
Sara: *A kiss… it's only a kiss, right?*
Sara: *I miss you.*

KY

MADISON'S PHONE ILLUMINATES her face, her eyebrows bunched in concentration. She looks up and smiles when she sees me approaching.

Once I'm in front of her, she pats my chair. I sit down and put my arm around her; she shifts beneath me until her front presses to my side and her hand rests on my stomach. "Ky?" she whispers.

I look down just in time to see the uncertainty in her eyes before her mouth settles on mine—and if it weren't for that split-second look I caught, I wouldn't have hesitated.

She must've noticed because she pulls back before I get a chance to speak and mumbles an apology.

"It's not you..." I shake my head at myself, feeling stupid for using such a cliché line. But it's the truth, it really isn't *just* her. It's both of us. "I'm not—"

"It's okay," she says, but her voice and her eyes tell me it's not. *She's hurt.* And I'm the one who hurt her.

"I'm serious, Madison. Any other time, any other place, I'd be all in." I take a calming breath before adding, "It's not that I don't want you. Believe me, I do. I just need to sort some shit out before—"

She takes my hand in hers, putting a pause on my rambling masterpiece. "It's fine, Ky. I understand."

I sigh again, louder, harsher, all while her sad eyes stay on mine.

Placing my hand behind her head, I bring her in and kiss her forehead. "Just..."

"What?" she asks, searching my eyes for answers.

She won't find them.

They don't exist.

It comes out a plea when I say, "Just...wait. Okay?" Please, I think, just wait until this bullshit with Jackson is over and I can give her what I really want.

She smiles—a genuine one that reaches her eyes.

We spend the rest of the movie in silence. Or at least it seems that way. But in my head, my jumbled thoughts are screaming, wanting to be heard.

Why the hell was DeLuca at my building?

I hold a hand to my chest, trying to ease the ache that's suddenly built.

"Are you okay?" Madison asks, her big, brown eyes peering up at me.

I swallow and wipe the sweat that's formed behind my neck. "I'm good."

"You're breathing erratically, and your heart's pounding. I can feel it against my cheek."

Squeezing my eyes, I try to calm my breathing—try to settle my pulse.

"Maybe you should get some air," she says.

I don't respond, but I don't have to—she's already on her feet, taking my hand to help me up.

Once we're out of the building and into the cold, I hold both her hands in mine to warm them. "I'm not crazy," I tell her.

"I didn't think you were."

She shivers slightly and I bring her into me, hugging her close.

"Was it the movie?" she asks.

I hadn't even been paying attention. "What?"

"The dad who died. The marine. Did it set off something for you?" she says, reaching up and fingering my tags.

"Yeah," I lie, because it's so much easier than telling her the truth.

Her arms wrap around me, and she hugs me back. "So what now?"

"Did you want to go home?"

She shakes her head. "What else did you have in mind?"

"I could do with a drink."

"Lead the way."

I take her hand and do as she asks; the entire time all I can think is that I'm a victim of my own past. A past I've spent too many years trying to escape. And now it's back... and the fucker's a ticking time bomb waiting to explode in my face.

11

KY

I TAKE HER to a bar a block away from our building. We both get carded at the door, and I show them my ID. She looks through her purse for a good five minutes before pouting up at the bouncer. He smiles, gives her a quick once over and lets her through. I get it—I'm not immune to that pout, either.

For a Wednesday night, the place is packed. There's only one seat free at the bar, so I let her take it and stand next to her. "What do you want to drink?"

She shrugs at first and then looks around at what other people are drinking. The bartender appears quickly and asks for our orders. "Do you need more time?" I ask her.

"Whiskey," Madison rushes out.

I raise my eyebrows at her. She does *not* look like the whiskey type.

"Single?" the dude asks.

"Double."

"Ice?"

She shakes her head, then looks at me for what seems like approval.

I shrug.

"Neat," she answers.

"And you?" the bartender asks.

"I'll have the same," I say, my eyes fixed on Madison. "You drink whiskey?"

She grimaces and nods slowly. "Is that bad?"

"No. It's *badass*. I hadn't pictured you the type."

Our drinks are placed in front of us, and after throwing some cash on the counter, I pick up the glasses and hand her one. She looks at the liquid, as if unsure. Then she closes her eyes and lifts the glass to her lips. She downs half of it before a small smile graces her face. She licks her top lip, slowly, from one side to the other. Then she does the same to the bottom, and I watch—captivated by her closed eyes, her lips, and her tongue—all while she makes a goddamn porno of drinking whiskey.

Then she does the worst possible thing my heart can handle.

She does it again.

And again.

And when she's done, she opens her eyes and catches me staring. "You don't like whiskey?" she asks, motioning to my untouched drink.

I lift the glass and swallow the entire thing, ignoring the alcohol both burning and warming my insides. "Another one?" I ask. I hope she says yes because I'd give just about anything to watch her performance again.

She nods.

I call the bartender and order another two.

And then we repeat the process.

She closes her eyes.

Makes love with her lips.

And all I can do is watch.

. . .

AFTER ANOTHER THREE rounds, my imagination can no longer handle the confines of my mind. Neither can my dick.

She leans into me, her body swaying—no doubt from the alcohol. Her mouth's on my neck, not kissing, not moving. Just *there*. I rest one arm on the counter, the other arm going around her waist and pulling her body against mine. The room spins. The voices around me are nothing but loud murmurs.

She whispers my name.

And I lose it.

I pull back just enough so I can see her face.

Her eyes are half-hooded.

"Madison?"

She looks up.

And then she smiles.

And I lose it all over again.

My mouth crashes down on hers, but she pushes me away. "Not here," she says, her eyes darting around us.

I don't care where. I just want her. So, I grab her hand and hold it all the way home—not just because I want to, but also because her unsteady feet *need* me to. By the time we get to our building, the alcohol has made its presence well and truly known.

Her chest heaves, matching mine, as we stare at each other on opposite sides of the elevator. I ball my fists and hold them behind my back—my only form of restraint from ripping her goddamn clothes off.

The whiskey's done its job, and I no longer feel the weight of my past—of everything—pressing down on my chest and choking the air out of me.

I feel free.

And I feel desire.

And lust.

And Madison.

All Madison.

I barely wait for the elevator doors to open, but when they do, I reach for her.

I go for her face.

She goes for my shirt.

We fumble with each other as we make our way to her door.

I pin her against it, my mouth claiming hers.

My hands are all over her while she tries to unlock her door. She retreats, just long enough to get the key in the hole and kick the door open. We enter in a daze. I slam it shut with my foot, my mouth never leaving hers. We trip over ourselves to get to her couch. Her ass hits the arm of it and she falls back, the back of her knees resting over it. I look down at her—at her chest rising and falling, her dress hitched up, revealing more of her creamy thighs. I groan and close my eyes, trying to fight the urge to spread her legs, drop to my knees and devour her...

"Ky!"

My eyes snap open. She's leaning up on her elbows now, watching me curiously. I blink a few times, willing the buzz of the alcohol and the uncontrollable lust to back the fuck off for just one second so I can calm the fuck down.

And then she licks her goddamn lips.

And that's all it takes.

I lose it.

My mouth covers hers.

Her legs wrap around mine.

I start to remove her sweater while she reaches for the buttons of my shirt, and we laugh, clumsily undressing each other. She moans when she undoes the last button of my shirt and her fingers lay flat on my stomach. I try to get her sweater past her elbows, but she's too busy fumbling with my belt. She leans up slightly, causing me to move back. I watch her face—her unfocused eyes and her overly exaggerated pout. Her lids are heavy as she curses, her eyebrows drawn, fixated on unfastening my belt.

Then she looks up at me, her chest heaving, and I stay still, waiting for her to finish.

"It won't..." she murmurs.

Her eyes flick to my belt and then back up at me.

And I see it now—an insecure innocence that has me questioning *everything*.

"Madison," I whisper.

"I just..."

I cover her hand with mine. "Madison," I say, louder, firmer.

With a shaky breath, she gazes back up at me.

I groan internally. "I can't believe I'm going to say this."

"What?" she breathes.

I let out a frustrated grunt. I'll regret it in the morning. Hell, I'll regret it in five seconds. "I should go home," I groan.

She yanks her hands away and sits taller. "What? Why?"

My eyes roam her face, down her incredible body, and back up again. *Yeah*, I'm already regretting it. "We've been drinking. You're drunk, and I don't want to take advantage of you."

"Oh," she whispers, dropping her gaze. She lifts her sweater back over her shoulders, hugging it tightly around her. "Okay." She gets off the couch but refuses to look at me.

"Madison?"

"No. You're right. This was..." She walks to her door and opens it for me, her gaze lowered. I stand in front of her and try to reach for her hand, but she yanks it away and holds it to her chest.

"Will you please look at me?" I beg.

"I can't."

"Why not?"

Her quiet whimper breaks through the deafening silence. "I'm so embarrassed right now. Can you just leave? Please."

I bend my knees to look in her eyes, and she moves her head to the side, avoiding me.

"Maddy, please don't be like this."

"I just need you to go."

MADISON

ALL THAT TIME wasted on cherishing the idea of a dinner and movie date…and this is what I get?

What a stupid cliché.

12

KY

Training this morning was a *whole* lot of fun.

Not.

I was pissed off and angry at the world.

Then Gunner made it worse by existing.

I took out my anger on him.

He looked terrified.

I wish I could say it helped, but it had zero effect.

Now, I am pacing my living room just like I've been doing for the past hour, and when enough time passes and I feel like I can actually think again, I open my door, take two steps to hers, and I knock.

Nothing.

Great. She's ignoring me.

I wait a few seconds before knocking again. This time her door opens, just enough so she can peek through it.

"Hi." I smile, hoping to God it's enough.

She doesn't return my smile. Instead, she looks down at her feet, her tone flat when she says, "What's up?"

"Can I come in?"

She shakes her head and opens the door wider—just slightly—before stepping out. "What's up?" she asks again.

My eyes narrow at her now-closed door. "You got someone in there?"

"What do you want, Ky?" she asks, her chin in the air like she's attempting to rein in whatever confidence I'd stripped from her last night.

And now she's avoiding my questions. *Fucking perfect.*

"I wanted to apologize."

"Is that it?"

I shrug. It's all I can do. "I guess."

She opens the door just enough to squeeze through, and without another word, I'm faced with yet another closed door.

There has to be someone in there. Someone she doesn't want me to see. Probably a guy she has on speed dial to physically take away the pain I'd caused.

I want to puke.

I don't.

Instead I go back in my apartment, shower, and make my way to stupid fucking therapy.

* * *

"How're things going with the girl?" is the first thing Dr. Aroma asks when I get in her office.

"They're not."

"Why not? Did something happen?"

"I think I'd like today to be one of those silent sessions where you just judge me and make me feel shittier than I already do."

She picks up her pen and notepad and starts scribbling.

I stare out the window.

This lasts an hour.

I tell her time's up.

She nods and waves goodbye.

And I go back to my self-pity and self-loathing.

13

KY

I FEEL AROUND my nightstand for my ringing phone, my eyes still closed and my body unwilling to wake up. When I finally find it, I hit answer and groan into it.

"Parker."

"DeLuca? What fucking time is it?"

Seconds of silence pass. "I need you to meet me. *Now.*"

"Where?" I ask, throwing the covers off of me and rubbing my eyes.

"I'll text you," he says, his tone clipped. He doesn't give me a chance to respond before hanging up, and when he does, I check the time. It's six in the goddamn morning. And now I'm officially pissed—I no longer have control of *anything* in my life, and now DeLuca feels he has the right to bark orders at me.

And I have no fucking choice but to obey.

* * *

"ARE YOU A cop?" DeLuca asks, taking a sip of his drink. We're sitting in a deli around the corner from my apartment.

It's completely empty, apart from the seedy-looking guy fucking around on his phone behind the counter.

I hadn't told Jackson I was meeting with DeLuca, and now I'm starting to regret it. "Do I look like a cop?"

DeLuca leans forward and narrows his eyes. "What's your story, Parker?"

"I'm between jobs," I say, attempting to sound bored.

"No. I mean, who are you? Have you got a wife? Kids? Pets? What makes you tick? What makes you wake up in the morning?"

Nothing. Absolutely nothing but a girl I can't get out of my goddamn head. With a sigh, I lean back in my chair, wanting him to get out of my space. "What's your point?"

"I don't trust you."

"I don't trust you, either, so I guess we're even."

He lifts a finger in the air, like he's about to gift me with his shitty words of wisdom. But what he says is: "You don't need to trust me. That's the thing, Ky. You're completely replaceable to me. That built-up rage you have—the one that's worked its way so deep inside you that you can't breathe—that's there forever. And you have no other outlet." He laughs mockingly. "I'm your ticket; *I'm* your outlet." He pauses a moment, tilting his head, letting his eyes bore into mine. "I'd love to know what happened to you. And I know it's not the war. No... that's not it. Not all of it, anyway. So what happened?" He smirks. "Did you fuck the wrong girl?"

My fingers ache from their grip on the side of my chair. It's the only thing holding me back from rushing across the table and treating his face like my personal punching bag.

His menacing chuckle fills my head with fury. "That's it, isn't it?" he continues, leaning forward again. "Or at least part of it. Is that why you enlisted—to get away from her? I bet you disappointed a lot of people when you left, huh? Your perfect parents. Your brothers and sisters?"

My jaw tightens.

He smiles. "Yeah, that's it. And *guilt.* I bet that guilt eats away at you, burning every last piece of your soul to the point where you'll never let yourself be happy. I bet—"

My chair scrapes across the floor as I stand and lunge for him.

But he's fast.

Too fast.

The cold metal of his gun presses against my forehead before I've even stood to full height.

DeLuca's eyes narrow, but they're calm.

Too fucking calm.

Fuck, I want to kill him.

Right here and now.

Bare hands.

Fuck the consequences.

"I *own* you now," he whispers before lowering the gun and shoving his hands in the front pocket of his sweatshirt. He lifts the hood over his head, straightens up, and casually walks out the door.

I eye the guy behind the counter, but he's too preoccupied with his phone to notice what just happened.

I let DeLuca fucking get to me.

And worse—I let him see my fear.

I've walked halfway back to my apartment before realizing that I have no fucking idea why DeLuca even wanted to meet. Was that his plan? To fuck with my head?

If so, it worked.

And I'm done playing his games.

I stand just outside the apartment doors and call Jackson, who answers first ring. "I saw that he called this morning. Are you meeting him?"

"I just did."

"You're supposed to tell me before you do anything. Have I not made it clear enough how dangerous this guy can be?"

"Probably not, but him holding a gun to my head just now may have done the trick."

"Fuck! Tell me you're joking."

"Jax, it's fine. I handled it." *Lie.* I'm still not handling it. "Can I ask you something?"

"Anything."

"Are you doing this for you or me?"

"What's the right answer here?"

"The truth, Jax."

"Both." He clears his throat. "Thank you, Ky."

"No need."

"Call Mom!" He hangs up.

I rub my eyes, hoping to hell this day will just end. When I open them, my heart drops to my stomach. Watching Madison walk from the elevator to the mailbox is like a sweet form of torture. Her hand shifts around the box and comes back empty. I find myself smiling, though I know I shouldn't, and when she turns around, catching me mid-stare, she does something completely unexpected. *She smiles.* And that smile remains as she walks to the door, her hips swaying from side to side.

I don't blink.

I don't move.

I'm in a trance, completely tangled in a web of nothing but Madison. For a moment, it feels right. And in that moment, I forget about the shit DeLuca just pulled.

She opens the door and sticks her head out, her eyes squinting from the little bit of sun peeking through the clouds. "Morning," she says, her voice smooth.

"Morning," I reply, trying to look her in the eyes. But I can't, because when I do, all I see is her pain—her pain and my regret.

She steps out of the doorway and stands a foot in front of me. "It's nice out," she says. "And I'm pretty sure you owe me a walk."

Relief washes through me. "I have somewhere to be," I tell her, and when her face falls, I quickly add, "But I'd love for you to join me."

She grins from ear-to-ear and settles her hand in the crook of my elbow. "Where are you taking me?"

She bounces on her toes as I lead us away, and instead of answering her question, I pull us to the side until her back is pressed against a building. "You okay?"

She looks up, confused. "What do you mean?"

"Not that I'm complaining, but after what happened I swore you'd never speak to me again, yet here we are..."

"I'm sorry," she says, but it comes out a question.

"You're sorry? I'm the one—"

She shakes her head quickly, cutting me off. "No, Ky. I was..." There's a hint of hesitation before she reaches out and links our hands. "I'm new... to whatever it is that's happening with you and me. You did the right thing. Honestly. It's just that, I guess I have a lot of self-doubts and very little self-confidence. So maybe I took it out of context—that's not your problem; it's mine. And I'm here because I want to try to work on it. And I'm hoping that maybe you can help me with that."

With a smile, I lean in close to her ear. "So if I tell you that I think you're beautiful, will that help?"

She nods slowly, a slight smile on her face, and it's all the answer I need. She says, "I like you, Ky, I really do..."

"As much as you like that mailbox?" I ask, hoping to steer her away from whatever rejection she's about to hand me.

It works, because she tosses her head back with her laugh.

"I have to admit, I do have a strong case of jealousy. If one day you wake up and there's a giant Hulk-smash fist through it, just know that it started it first."

She smiles. "So, friends?" she asks.

"Friends," I agree, and as the word leaves my mouth, I hadn't expected it to feel so right.

I need a friend, a distraction from everything else. She could totally be my distraction. I hold her hand and continue our walk.

"Are you going to tell me where we're going?"

"We're here." I stop to open the door of Debbie's Flowers and wait until she steps inside, and when she does, she freezes immediately, her hands at her sides. Then she inhales deeply, her eyes closed and her smile getting wider with each passing second.

All I can do is stare, fascinated by her reaction. It's as if she's just gained the sense of smell and is appreciating it for the first time. She inhales twice more before finally opening her eyes. "It's beautiful," she whispers, and somehow I find myself smiling with her.

"What can I help you with?" the older woman behind the counter asks.

I take Madison's hand and lead her there, pulling out my credit card at the same time. "I need to get a dozen white lilies delivered, please."

The woman smiles at Madison first and then at me. "This is the third time you've been in here. I remember your order." Not in the mood for small talk, I hand over my card and give the old lady the delivery details. "This isn't for her?" the woman asks, nodding her head at Madison. I look down at her nametag: *Debbie*, of course.

"No, ma'am."

Madison releases my hand and starts to walk around the

store while Debbie gets the order ready. I use the time that Madison's distracted to purchase something extra. Something small. Something hers.

MADISON

"Give me your keys," Ky says as we enter our building.

I stop and face him. "What?"

With his hand out, palm up, he motions toward it.

I hesitate for a second before reaching into my bag and finding the keys. His eyes light up, matching the goofy grin on his handsome face. "Turn around," he orders.

"What?"

"Turn around," he repeats, louder and firmer.

I do as he asks.

His footsteps move farther away, right before I hear the lock turning in a mailbox. He comes back a moment later and drops the keys in my bag, then grabs my hand. "Let's go!"

I look longingly at my mailbox while he drags me to the elevator. "But—"

He cuts me off. "It's the element of surprise, remember?"

I dig my heels in the floor and grasp his hand tighter. Looking into his eyes, I suppress my smile when I tell him, "I can't wait." Slowly, I back away from him and move closer to the mailboxes.

He sighs and shakes his head, but he's smiling as his eyes fixate on mine. I wonder if he can see my excitement, because I'm sure having a hard time containing it. My fingers shake when I place the key in the lock, the anticipation bursting out of me. I stop to take a breath, then another, as I try to calm myself down, try to savor this moment.

Ky comes up behind me and places his hands on my waist, the warmth of it causing my heart to race. He dips his mouth to my ear. "Go ahead."

I don't hesitate this time. I open the box, reach in, and pull out the single short-stemmed yellow rose. My breath catches on a gasp, too many emotions hitting me at once. I push them all back and take a moment to gather my thoughts. Then I lift the rose to my nose and inhale deeply. Tears fill my eyes, but I don't care. I turn to him, a million voices in my head wanting to tell him *everything*. Instead, I lower the rose and let him see *me*. "Thank you, Ky."

He nods in response. "Yellow roses—the flower of *friendship*."

14

KY

TAPPING HER PEN on her notepad, Dr. Aroma eyes me curiously. "I'd love to play this little guessing game, but I have a feeling it'll be easier if you just tell me what it is that has you a little more relaxed and smiling today."

"I'm not smiling," I say defensively.

"Well," she says, "you're not exactly pissed at the world like you were last time."

I roll my eyes. "Do all girls like flowers?"

She sets her pen and notepad on the seat next to her. "What's her name?"

"Madison."

"And you want to give her flowers?"

I shrug.

She laughs a little. "Most girls do. Tell me about her?"

"She's... different, I guess."

"How?"

"I don't know," I tell her, the uncertainty in my voice evident. "She's kind of hot as fuck, but she doesn't know it. Makes her hotter, you know?"

Smiling, she asks, "Has Jax met her?"

"Who?" I tease.

Her face falls and she clears her throat, squirming in her seat as she attempts to rein in a level of professionalism. "I mean Detective Davis."

I raise an eyebrow at her slip-up. "How well do you know Jax?"

"Time's up."

* * *

THERE'S A KNOCK on my door. It's quiet. Timid, almost. Which only means one thing, and that one thing has me grinning like an idiot. Madison stands on the other side with a pizza in her hands. "Your place or mine?"

I open the door wider for her. We'd only been apart for a couple of hours, and I was already looking forward to seeing her again. Taking the pizza box from her, I set it on the coffee table and link both her hands in mine.

We stare at each other, trying to contain our matching smiles.

"You missed me, huh?" I ask.

"I was hungry."

Laughing, I lead her to the couch, pulling her down with me and scooting her ass as close as possible.

She faces me. "Can I ask you something?"

"Sure."

"The flowers—"

My instant smirk cuts her off.

"Why are you looking at me like that?"

"You want to know who they were for?" I can't wipe the smug smile off my face. "Are you jealous?"

"No!" she all but shouts.

"My mom. Well, my foster mom. Kind of. They're for

her," I admit. "I've been sending her flowers once a month since her husband passed away five years ago."

"You call her your mom?"

I shrug. "She's the closest thing I have to the real thing."

"That's sweet."

I take one of her hands and trace lazy circles on her palm. "So Jeff... he used to come home with them once a month on the date of their anniversary. White lilies were their wedding flower. Today's their monthly wedding anniversary." I smile to myself, lost in my thoughts, in my memories of them. "It was kind of beautiful... the way they were. I'd never really witnessed what love was until they took me in."

"That *is* beautiful," she whispers. "And I'm sorry about Jeff but..." she trails off.

"But what?"

"Nothing. I'm just nosy."

"No. What were you going to say?"

She straightens up, as if preparing for battle. "It's just that I saw a sign at the shop and it said *local delivery only*...so she's local, right? Why not just give them to her?"

I release an anxious breath, trying to find the right words. "I haven't spoken to her since I was eighteen. I doubt she even knows they're from me."

"So who would she think they're from?"

A single laugh escapes me. "Probably Jackson."

"Jackson?"

I lift my gaze to hers. She's concentrating on my finger tracing her palm. "Her son."

"Do you keep in touch with him?"

"We just started talking again...."

She looks up from her hand—her eyes now focused on mine. "Did you miss him?"

"Yeah. I really did."

KY: AGE SEVENTEEN

I LOCKED MYSELF *in my room for three days. Three days I didn't see Jackson or Christine. And in those three days, Jackson became our rock, our strength. I don't know how he did it—but he must've known we needed saving, or at least knew Christine did. Me though? He had no fucking clue how badly I needed someone—something—to take my pain away.*

A knock on my door made me groan. "Go away."

Jackson entered anyway and opened the curtains, letting sunlight into the room. It'd been three days since I'd seen it, and it made me want to puke. I threw a pillow at his head. He ducked it and told me to fuck off—a well-earned response. "Are you okay, Ky?"

I sighed and lifted the covers over my head. What was I going to say? That the only man I'd ever looked up to was gone, and my girlfriend that I needed at the time needed someone else more?

"Mom—" Jackson started.

"Has she been asking for me?" I cut in.

My bed dipped when he sat on the edge. "No. But she's not in a good way, Ky."

"She'll get over it. We all will." And even as the words left my mouth, I knew it was harsh. And I knew that it was a lie. How do you get over losing someone you love? How do you stop missing them?

"So..." Jackson said, and I could hear the hesitation in his voice. I knew what was coming before he spoke. "Did something happen with Ashlee?"

I couldn't speak.

"It's just that she hasn't been around to see you or Mom. I thought for sure she'd be here..." he trailed off.

I sunk further into the bed. "Can you close the curtains and leave, please?"

He exhaled loudly and got off the bed. Curtains scraped across the rod followed by heavy footsteps moving toward the door. "Jax?" I lifted the covers and faced him.

Jackson froze with his hand on the knob. "Yeah, Ky?" His voice was so quiet, so low, so damn sad I wanted to cry for him.

"Thank you."

He turned around slowly and leaned against the door, staring down at his feet. Shoving his hands in his pockets, he shrugged. And then he frowned. I hated it, because I knew what it meant—pity. "It's no problem, Ky. You're my brother. You saved me." He let out a sad laugh and finally looked up at me. "Maybe now you can let me save you?"

I ducked under the covers to shield him from my tears.

A few seconds later, I heard the door click shut.

"KY?"

I blink and push back the memories.

"Where did you go just now?" Madison asks.

"Sorry. Spaced out."

She gives me an unsure smile. "So Jackson?"

"Yeah, what about him?"

"Can I meet him?"

I raise my eyebrows. "Already wanting to meet the family? A little soon, don't you think?"

"I just want to get to know you more. That's all."

"He's busy a lot. I doubt he'll have time."

"Sure you're not just ashamed to be seen with me?"

"No." I laugh. "More like I want to keep you to myself. What if you fall for him? Then what?"

She ignores me and grabs my phone off the coffee table. "Ask him."

I'm about to argue, but her face is set with determination and I can't say no.

She kicks my leg with her bare feet. "Come on, Kyler, what's the worst he can say? No? He's too busy?"

"I'll call him if you promise never to call me Kyler again."
"Deal, *Kyler.*"

Ky: *Madison wants to meet you.*
Jackson: *Madison?*
Ky: *My neighbor.*

I stare at the phone a moment, waiting for a reply. When it doesn't come after a minute, I set it back on the table.

"What did he say?" she asks.

"Hasn't replied." To be honest, I'm a little disappointed. As much as I don't want Madison involved in what Jax and I are doing, I want my brother to meet the girl I'm into, and I want his approval... almost to the point where I *need* it. Because I want to give him a reason to be proud of me again. And right now, Madison's the only thing I have to be proud of. I'd almost given up hope when a message comes through.

Jackson: *When?*
I look at Madison. "When?"
Her smile is instant. "Right now!"
"*Now?*"
"No wasting time, Ky, remember?"

Ky: *She said now.*
Jackson: *Whipped already? Nice job. I'm at O'Malley's bar checking out the place. Meet me here in thirty? I'll hand you back your balls when you guys get here.*

"You ready?" I ask her.

Her eyes go huge. "Okay!" She shoots to her feet. "I'll just freshen up."

Five minutes later, she knocks on my door—barefoot, hair a mess, wearing a bathrobe. "You're going like that?" I ask.

She pulls on my arm and drags me through her apartment and into her room.

Clothes.

Everywhere.

She's either the messiest girl I've ever met or she's just been robbed.

"I don't know what to wear!" she rushes out. "I was so excited to meet your brother, and now I'm panicking because I don't know what to wear! What do you wear when you go to meet your prospective—" She cuts herself off, takes a deep breath, and then starts again. "Where are we even meeting? What's the dress code? Does he like casual or proper? Will he look down on me if I—what if he doesn't like me and then he tells you and—"

I lose it in a fit of laughter.

"This isn't funny, Ky!"

I reel it in, just enough so that I can grab her shoulders and sit her on the edge of her bed. "Maddy... he's going to like you because *I* like you and because it's kind of impossible not to like you. He won't care what you wear because he's not like that. If you want me to call him and cancel I will, but you're overthinking it. I promise."

After taking a few calming breaths, she yells, "Get out!"

I flinch.

She shoos me away. "I need to get dressed! Get out!"

* * *

MADISON CHOOSES ANOTHER modest dress, which is good because I'm really not in the mood to be punching creeps that look at her the wrong way, especially in front of my detective brother.

I point to Jackson once we're in the bar. He's sitting in a corner booth, dressed casually, sipping a beer while checking his phone. I can tell she's nervous because her grip on my hand tightens with each step we take. "Jackson," I say, standing next to the table.

He looks up, smiling when he sees me, but the smile doubles when he sees Maddy. He stands up and gives me the standard bro hug. I don't miss his quick once-over of Madison when he turns to her. "You must be Madison?"

"And you're Jackson?" she replies, throwing her hand out for a shake. He ignores her hand and goes in for a hug. A nice, long, tight, semi-inappropriate hug. He winks at me over her shoulder and murmurs in her ear, "You smell so good."

"All right." I step forward and peel him off of her while he tries to hide his amusement. "That's enough of that."

He gives her one more squeeze before letting go.

"You're an ass," I tell him, gesturing for Maddy to take a seat. Jax chuckles. "You guys need drinks?"

"I got it," I say quickly.

"Shut up, Parker. It's on me."

"No."

"Yes."

"No, I said—"

"You trying to show off?"

"No. I can buy—"

"Boys!" Maddy interrupts. "You can *both* go."

Jax and I laugh.

"Fine," he says.

I smile down at her. "Are you good?"

She nods.

I give her a quick kiss on her temple, then follow Jax to the bar. He orders a round of beers and then turns back to look at Madison.

I do the same. "Thanks for meeting us, man. I know how you feel about her being around—"

"So she just asked you if she could meet me?" he interrupts.

I shrug, my eyes fixed on her. "Yeah, I told her about you and—"

"How much does she know?"

"Relax. I just told her I had a brother. That's all."

He exhales loudly. "It's been six years, Ky. You and I are still brothers?"

"It's been five, Jax, and we'll always be brothers."

"I'm sorry," he says. "I've kind of been an asshole. I dragged your ass into this and gave you no choice."

"Jax, this means more to me than you—"

"Maybe," he cuts in. "I just don't want anything getting between us this time. Our relationship comes first, Ky. If the case gets in the way, we call the whole thing off."

I clear the lump in my throat, unable to respond.

He adds, "She seems nice. I'm happy for you."

"She's amazing, Jax." Before he gets a chance to respond, the bartender gets our attention. I turn to him and throw a twenty on the bar before Jackson can stop me. Picking up all three beers, I face Jackson, but he's staring at our table, eyes narrowed, jaw clenched.

I follow his gaze and my heart stops. Along with everything else.

Opposite Madison, sitting in Jackson's seat, is Nate DeLuca, with his forearms resting on the table as he leans into her. His mouth moves, and whatever he's saying has her smiling.

"Don't let him take it," Jax says.

"Take what?" I ask, my eyes never leaving them.

"*You*. You told me that, remember? Don't let him *own* you." He pats my shoulder. "Tell her I got a call and had to leave. Go deal with him. And Ky?"

"Yeah?"

"Remember what I said. Become his friend. Get in his head. We need to know everything about him. It's the only way we can *ruin* him."

"And the only way we get revenge, right?"

"Like I said, if it's not worth it for you, just say the word."

"I'll call you. Get out of here."

* * *

THE BEERS LAND on the table with a thud. I look at Madison first; she smiles, assuring me that she's fine. Then I switch my attention to DeLuca.

"Well, if it isn't my old friend Parker. I was just telling—"

"Let's talk," I cut in.

He leans back, stretching his arms across the top of the seat. "I'm right here."

It takes everything in me to resist wrapping my hands around his throat until he's blue in the fucking face. Leaning down, I quietly speak in his ear. "You made your point this morning. You won, okay? Don't make a scene. Not here. Not now." When I pull back, I notice his focus is on Madison again. Without a word, he braces his hands on the table and stands up. Then he leads me to the corner of the bar, where he leans against the wall but never takes his eyes of Madison.

"Listen," I start, then sigh, trying to find the words. "I don't know what you want from me, but whatever it is, I'll give it to you. Like you said, I need to prove myself, right?"

His eyes move to mine as he crosses his arms and nods once.

"From the beginning, you told me how it was, and maybe I haven't been treating you with the respect you deserve. I'll fix it. We need to make this work. You know I want to fight. You know I *need* to fight," I tell him.

A cocky smirk takes over his face.

My fists ball at my sides, but I rein it in. "Just please leave her out of it. I don't want her involved, and I don't want her to see this side of me. I need to protect her from all of this." It's all a lie. Everything but how I feel about Madison.

His smirk disappears, replaced with something I can't decipher. His eyes trail back to Madison as he mumbles, "Okay, man. Fresh start." He throws out his hand, and I force myself to shake it. He adds, "We start tonight," as he kicks off the wall. He makes his way over to our table and sits back down. And I have no fucking choice but to let him.

"Everything okay?" Madison asks when I'm sitting next to her again.

"It's fine." I pick up her hand and kiss her palm, then hold it on the table so DeLuca understands I'm not fucking around, especially when it comes to Madison. "DeLuca, this is Madison—Madison, DeLuca."

"Madison," he says, but it comes out a question. She nods, her lips pursed as his gaze flicks to our joined hands again. Then he rubs his thumb across his bottom lip and looks back up at her. "Well, Madison, you can call me Nate."

She fakes a smile and squeezes my hand to get my attention. "We didn't eat. I'm a little hungry."

DeLuca raises his hand to get the waiter's attention. "They have awesome burgers here."

"Where's Jackson?" she asks me.

"He got a call. Emergency. Had to leave."

"That sucks. We'll have to catch up with him again soon."

DeLuca orders our burgers and spends the next ten minutes ignoring me and giving Madison his full attention. He asks her questions I'd never thought to ask. Like what TV shows she watches, what music she's listening to, if she likes any restaurants or take-out joints in our area. She answers each one enthusiastically, and he listens to her intently. Their conversation ends when the food arrives. "Oh my god," Madison mumbles. "This looks *so* good!"

I laugh, watching her pick up the burger and bring it to her mouth. "This tastes amazing, Ky," she moans. She picks up a napkin and covers her mouth while she finishes chewing. "Where have you been all my life?" she says to the burger.

I glance over at DeLuca, but he isn't laughing. He's staring right at her, *frowning*.

I clear my throat to get his attention, and his eyes snap to mine. He glimpses once more at Madison before standing up. "I'll leave you guys to it." He throws a wad of cash on the table and says, "I'll call you, Parker." Then to Madison, "It's been an absolute pleasure." And then he walks away, leaving his plate completely untouched.

15

KY

I KNOW IT'S Madison knocking without having to open the door. She has this specific knock. Three taps. All quiet. All timid. Kind of like her.

I open the door with a smile—one that she returns. "You're crazy about me, aren't you?" I tease.

With a shrug, she pushes past me and makes herself comfortable on the couch. "How was the gym?" she asks.

"I got slaughtered," I tell her truthfully. After taking my anger out on Gunner a few days ago, he'd decided to pay me back. Only he, or maybe even DeLuca, felt it necessary to call in a favor. I recognized the guy from one of the many pictures hanging on the gym walls. He told me his next fight was set a month from now as a contender for the UFC middleweight title. He was a weight class below me, but that didn't matter. He sure as fuck made it known that he was better than me, and I had no choice but to accept it.

Gunner—he loved every damn second of it. So did DeLuca as he half watched from the sidelines, too busy switching from his laptop to his phone to pay full attention.

I called Jax when I was done and told him about it. "We need to get access to his computer," he said. "Whatever he's doing on there—that's our ticket." I told him that it was on him at all times, and when it wasn't, it was locked up and with Tiny. That got him excited. "Leave it to me," he said, before hanging up.

"You look fine," Madison says, bringing me back to the present. Her brow bunches as she looks me up and down.

"Yeah?" I make my way over to her. "You should see my ribs."

She sits up a little straighter. "Show me."

I lift my shirt, revealing what's no doubt the beginning of some heavy-set bruises.

"You need to ice it..." she murmurs, reaching up and using the back of her fingers to slowly skim across the sensitive areas. They move past my ribs and down to my stomach. She chews her lip as her single finger traces the dips of my abs, her mouth parting slightly and her eyes fixed on our contact. Her breaths are short now, coming out in tiny spurts. I focus on her breasts as they heave up and down, up and down... In reality, it's only a few seconds, but the warmth of her hand on my bare skin amplifies each and every one. Then she blinks and, as if realizing what she's been doing, yanks her hand away. "Ice," she whispers, getting up and moving to the fridge. When she returns, I'm already sitting on the couch, my shirt off, waiting for her. She hands me an ice pack and moves far, far away from me. So far, she's at the front door again. "I'll come back later."

"No, stay," I rush out. "Give me ten minutes to ice, five to shower, and we can head out."

"Why do you do it? Train to fight, I mean."

The first time she asked what I did with my days, I hesitated to tell her the truth. But I figured if I just told her what

I did and kept the reason to myself, it would be enough. And it was. Until now. I let out a pained groan and ignore her question. "What did you have planned for today?"

"So you're not going to tell me *why?*"

I sigh and motion for her to sit back down next to me, giving me time to come up with a response.

"So?" she asks once she's settled on the couch again.

"I have some issues I'm dealing with," I tell her, which isn't too far from the truth. "Punching things in a controlled environment—it helps clear my head."

She stares me down, probably deciding whether or not to run, but after a while, her shoulders lift with her shrug. "Anything you want to do today?"

I release a breath, relieved that it's enough. "You know I'm happy as long as I'm with you." So I'm turning up my charm, but it's not a lie. This has been our routine for the past three days since that shit happened with DeLuca—I hit the gym for a few hours in the mornings, then I come home, and a few minutes later she'll knock on my door. We spend the next few hours doing whatever she wants until I have to leave for therapy or another gym session. Then we repeat the process. Only we have dinner together—somewhere new every night. She seems to like exploring downtown and the different varieties of food on every street corner.

Yesterday, when I got back from my morning training session, she was waiting for me in the lobby, and I loved that she was. I asked her what she'd been doing, and she told me she'd just been waiting for me. That thought alone had me wanting to hit the emergency stop button on the elevator and pin her to the wall to flood her with gropes and kisses.

I didn't.

Later on, she admitted that she had a hard time leaving the apartment alone. She said she had anxiety in crowds and felt safe with me but didn't elaborate further and changed the subject.

She did that a lot, I noticed.

We don't do much as far as activity—she just loves being outside, regardless of what we're doing. And she likes to *breathe*—as weird as it sounds. I have no other way of explaining it. When we're out, I often catch her stopping just to take a breath. Sometimes it's to smell the air, but other times, it seems like she's just appreciating the ability to breathe.

To anyone else, she might seem a little crazy. To me— she's kind of breathtaking. *Literally.* She also asks a lot of questions but doesn't offer much in return. And I think I'm okay with that... for now.

"So do you actually enjoy training?" she asks, pulling me out of my daze.

I shrug, moving the ice pack to my other side. "It keeps me in check. Keeps me disciplined."

"How long were you deployed for?"

"I did four deployments, so four years."

"Do you ever feel like it's too much? The freedom?"

I look at her, but her eyes are cast downward. "What do you mean?"

She shakes her head before lifting her gaze. "Nothing. I'll be in my apartment. Just come get me when you're done."

MADISON

Madison: *I'm having a really bad day.*
Sara: *What's wrong? Did something happen?*
Madison: *No. Nothing happened. I just feel so lost.*
Sara: *Are you taking your meds?*
Madison: *Yes.*

* * *

I OPEN THE door, wiping tears from my cheeks.

"Hey," Ky says, bringing me into him. "What's wrong?"

The sympathy in his voice makes me cry harder. "Nothing," I tell him, because I wouldn't even know where to begin. I take a deep breath and square my shoulders. "I'm fine," I lie. He pushes me back a little so he can look in my eyes. I fake a smile, not wanting him to be affected by my mood. "Seriously, I'm fine."

His brow pinches. "Is it me?"

"No!" I say quickly. "Not at all."

"Then what is it?"

I walk to the fridge and pull out a bottle of water. "You ever have one of those days when it's just... the colors are dull and even the fresh air seems suffocating?" It sounds stupid, even to me. I lean against the counter, my eyes on the floor. "I'm just having one of those days."

He stops in front of me and grips the counter on either side of me. "So let's brighten your day."

I want to laugh. "I wish it were that easy."

"Who says it can't be?" he asks.

He sounds so hopeful I can't help but look up at him. "What did you have in mind?"

"Are you ready to go now?"

Sighing, I let my shoulders slump. "We don't have to do anything, Ky. We can just stay in."

He smiles. "I'm not a fan of wasting time, Madison. There's too much in the world. Too much to see. Too much to do. Too much to *breathe*. We miss it all if we just stay in our apartments all day."

I smile as he repeats my words from a few days ago. "So what are we doing?"

"Element of surprise, remember?"

* * *

DEBBIE WALKS TOWARD us with a huge smile on her face.

"Kyler," she sings. "It's good to see you again."

"So she's allowed to call you Kyler but I'm not?"

He squeezes my hand in response.

"What are we doing here, anyway?"

Ignoring me, he holds my hand tighter and leads us to follow behind Debbie, and as soon as I step foot in the back of the store, I gasp and dig my heels in the floor. My eyes dart everywhere, all at once. It's a flower warehouse and the smell... oh my God, *the smell*. I close my eyes and inhale deeply, taking it all in. It's been years since my senses have had so much to take in.

"Is the air still suffocating?" Ky whispers, his breath warm against my cheek.

I shake my head in disbelief and open my eyes to see him watching me. "Not at all, Ky."

"Kyler," Debbie shouts, poking her head out from behind a row of pots. "You coming?"

"Yeah!" He drags me toward her.

"Here it is." Debbie points to a large potted plant. "It's not exactly how it was pictured online," she mumbles, sounding disappointed.

"It's perfect," Ky assures her.

I move in front of him so I can see what they're talking about. "It's beautiful."

Debbie lifts the plant to my nose. "You should smell it."

Ky settles his hand on my shoulder while I dip my head, my chest rising with my intake of breath. It smells just as beautiful as it looks, and I tell Ky that when I look up at him, hoping he understands everything my eyes are trying to convey; that I appreciate him and that what he's doing means more to me than he'll ever know. Because he's giving me a part of my life back, a life I thought I'd lost.

"Want to know what it is?" Debbie asks me.

"Yes."

"They're rainbow roses. They fuse together all the different colors, and it comes out like this. Kyler gave you a yellow one, yes?"

I nod.

Debbie smiles. "It's the flower of friendship."

I place my hand over his settled on my shoulder. "So I've been told."

"Well," Debbie says, inspecting the flower. "Kyler wanted to give you one that represented all the things. This one has a little of everything." Debbie looks up at Ky. "Dark pink for thankfulness, orange for fascination, peach for modesty." She moves her gaze back to me. "Red and orange for love and desire."

Ky chokes on a gasp.

I giggle like a schoolgirl.

Debbie adds, "I was thinking of giving it a nickname for the store. I don't much like Rainbow Rose. Any suggestion?"

"Madison," Ky says from above me.

"Yeah?"

He laughs. "No. Madison. The name. You should call it Madison."

"Perfect," Debbie says. "It suits. Beautiful name for a beautiful flower to match the beautiful girl."

Ky chuckles. "Wow, Debbie. You're doing all the hard work for me."

There's an ache in my chest that's anchored its way to my stomach, holding my response captive, and I can't seem to do a thing.

Why? Why was it so easy for him to see through me? To feel every part of me? To know how to take my pain and my fears and make them disappear. Why was it so easy to make me fall for him?

"Madison?" he asks, turning me to him. "Are you crying?"

I didn't realize I was. "Why would you do that, Ky?"

"Because you don't deserve to live in a world without color."

16

KY

"So I KIND of gave her flowers," I tell Dr. Aroma.

"Oh yeah?" she says through a smile. "And how did she react?"

"She smiled."

"That's a good outcome."

"We haven't picked it up yet. It's still at the shop getting monitored."

Her eyebrows lift. "So I take it they're not just standard flowers. What are they?"

"Madisons."

"Like her name?" she asks.

"Yep."

"And you—you're smiling, too."

I shrug. "I guess I like making her happy."

"Just her?"

"What do you mean?"

She leans forward a little. "You just seem like the kind of guy who likes to please people. Are you a people pleaser, Ky?"

I shrug again, then I laugh. "She makes me want to please myself."

She laughs with me, understanding my hidden meaning. "She not pleasing you in that way?"

"Time's up."

* * *

WE'VE JUST FINISHED checking on the Madison and are a block away from our building when she stops in front of a dollar store. "What is this place?" she asks.

"Seriously?"

She nods.

"It's just a shop full of cheap junk."

"That sounds fun." Before I know it, she has my arm in a death grip and is dragging me into the store, where we spend a good ten minutes messing around with all the crap they have inside. She tries on about fifty different pairs of sunglasses before choosing a bright yellow pair. "For friendship," she says, and I laugh at how goofy they look on her. At some point, we get separated and I find her staring at a bunch of picture frames, her finger tracing each one, inspecting them.

I stand next to her. "You want to get one?"

"I don't know which one."

She lifts one off the rack and looks intently at it. It's chrome with the word 'Love' printed on the bottom, but she doesn't seem to be looking at the frame; she's looking at the picture inside it.

"You know you're meant to change it, right? Or are you into the dude in the picture?" I ask, only half joking.

She doesn't respond. It's as if she hasn't even heard me. "Look at them," she says quietly.

I look down at the couple in the picture, who are standing in front of a fountain facing each other. The girl has her arms around the guy's neck; his hands are around her waist and they're just staring at each other, smiling. "Can you imagine what that would feel like?" she asks.

My heart tightens at the sincere sadness in her tone. "What do you mean?" I ask, my eyes on hers. I press on when she seems not to have heard me. "Can I imagine what it feels like to be in love?"

She shakes her head. "No. Not just love... but to be so open about it. To love so freely... like it doesn't matter if anyone's watching," she whispers, tears beginning to fill her eyes.

"Madison," I whisper, and she looks up at me. I hold the side of her face, my eyes on hers, and I plead with her to give me something... anything... so that maybe I can understand what the hell is happening right now.

But I don't understand.

I can't.

So I do the only thing I can do. I lean down, press my lips to hers, and I kiss her. She gasps, taking my breath with her, and after a second, her lips move, her free hand gripping my shirt as I bring her in closer. Her breath catches when our tongues meet, sliding agonizingly slowly against each other and I hesitate, my heart pounding painfully against my chest, because *dammit* I'm nervous.

And I'm so fucking afraid of everything the kiss makes me feel.

Because it's more than just a kiss.

It's a sense of hope, and reason, and *promise*.

She quickly steps back, as if suddenly realizing where we are and what we're doing, while I finally allow myself to breathe. I open my eyes to see her watching me, her chest heaving with each breath.

"Shit." It's all I can get out—the only word that forms in my head.

"I think I'm going to buy this one," she says, reaching up and grabbing another frame. "And this one."

* * *

I STEP INTO her apartment when she opens the door, not bothering to wait for an invitation. Not that she seems to mind. She goes straight to the couch and pulls out the frames from the bag and sets them on the coffee table in front of her. I sit next to her, not knowing what else to do. She didn't speak much on the walk home, and I didn't want to push her. Truth is, I'm still thinking about that kiss. Watching her now, though, it's clear she's still thinking about that damn picture because she's staring at it intently, her brow creased. "How do you think they met?"

I look at the frame. "The couple?"

"Yeah."

"Probably the day of the photo shoot..."

She nudges my side and pulls on my elbow until my arm settles on her leg. "Come on, Ky. Just play along. Please?"

"Fine." I look back at the picture. "He probably walked into his apartment building and saw her kicking the shit out of the mailboxes."

She cackles with laughter. "And it turned out that they live opposite each other," she muses.

"And he thought she was smokin' hot, so he brought over pizza."

"After he unintentionally made her feel like an idiot for not knowing about the maintenance guy when she locked herself out."

"Yeah," I say, all amusement leaving me. "But he was hoping the pizza made up for all that."

"Not the pizza," she says, all playfulness gone, "but the message behind it."

"So the girl knew he was interested in getting to know her?"

"No. Not at the pizza stage, but then he gave her a yellow rose—a symbol of friendship—and after that she kind of knew."

I face her. "Well, I'm glad they were on the same page."

She smiles, but her eyes remain on the frame. "And then what happened?"

"Then I guess the guy was just happy because he figured the girl missed him when he wasn't around and, for some reason, she always wanted to be around him. I'm pretty sure that made him feel like the luckiest guy in the world."

She holds my arm tighter. "Yeah? I think it might be the other way around. I think that maybe the girl's lucky. After all, he did name a flower after her."

"So what happened after?"

Her smile falls, along with her gaze. "They kissed."

"And it was bad?"

She finally turns to me, shaking her head. "Not for her."

"Not for him, either, Maddy."

She rests her head on my shoulder, her exhales warming my neck. Then I feel it—her lips on my skin. I tense beneath her touch, and she kisses me once, soft and wet. She whispers, "It's just a story, Ky. It could be fake."

I pull back slightly and rest my forehead on hers, my heart pounding way too hard, way too fast. "Is it, though? Fake?"

She doesn't respond with words. She doesn't have to. Her lips find mine, gentle at first, then all at once, we lose the control we've been holding on to for days.

We stop resisting and we give in—to each other and to the inevitable.

My mouth covers hers as she presses on my chest, pushing me until I'm on my back. Our breaths mingle, our hands everywhere at once. Our lips lock, only parting long enough

to gasp for breath before we're back, kissing, touching, grop-
ing. She's on top of me now, a leg on either side of my hips.

She's grinding.

I'm thrusting.

She's moaning.

I'm groaning.

But we're synced.

In.

Every.

Single.

Possible.

Way.

I find the bottom of her dress, my fingers curling around
the soft material, and once my hands make their way to her
ass, she emits the sexiest sound I've ever heard in my entire
goddamn life. I curse into her mouth, feeling my cock throb
in the confines of my jeans while her fingers lace in my hair,
gripping lightly as she grinds harder into me. Her movements—her sounds—all of it pushes me to the edge of
explosion.

I pull back just in time. "Maddy."

Her eyes snap open. They're huge. "Huh?" She looks so
damn confused.

"I want more. Of you. Of us. Of all of this." I swallow
nervously, trying to catch my breath. She stays silent while I
anticipate her response.

Each second I wait, my confidence fades.

"So..." She looks nervously everywhere but at me. "You're
asking for sex?"

I shake my head. "I don't just want you physically, Maddy.
I don't just want your body. I want *all* of you."

"Okay," she whimpers.

I reach up and pull her mouth back to mine. I kiss her
gently until she lets out a sob, completely confusing me. Her

hot and cold, her sweet innocence and then her complete and utter lust—it fucks with my head.

And then it hits me…"Madison? Are you a virgin?"

She shakes her head.

My heart thumps faster, not from excitement, but from fear. I ask, even though I may not want the answer. "Did someone force—"

"No," she cuts in quickly. "I just…" she trails off and sits up, biting her lip as she runs a hand down my stomach, past my waist and skims the bulge in my pants. Her eyes lift to mine before she stands up and grabs my hand, helping me up. She leads me to her bedroom and closes the door behind her before switching on the light on her nightstand. I sit on the edge of her bed, my heart racing as she removes her sweater. Then she stands in front of me, her legs between mine, and I reach out, cupping the back of her knees to bring her closer to me. Her hands cover my jaw, tilting my head up to look at her. "I want you, too, Ky," she says. "I'm just not ready to give you all of me. Not yet."

I nod. I'll take anything as long as she's *mine*.

She swallows loudly, pushing the straps of her dress down her shoulders and lets the material slide down her arms, then her chest. I bite my fist, trying to contain my moan. "Fuck." I groan when the fabric passes her tits, revealing her black lace bra. I lick my lips, adjusting myself at the same time. I think she's about to stop—to put the moment on pause—and I don't know how much more I can handle. But then her hands rise, thumbing the material around her waist… and then she pushes down, lower and lower.

Matching. Goddamn. Panties.

I can't speak.

I can't swallow.

I can't fucking breathe.

"Is this… am I okay?" she asks, her hands at her sides.

I lean forward, wrapping my arm around her waist, and I pull her to me. I kiss her stomach, just above her navel. She sways into me, her hands on my shoulders helping her balance, while my mouth moves higher until it covers her breast, biting gently on her bra-covered nipple. "You're fucking perfect, Maddy." I reach behind her, fingering the clasp of her bra and praying to everything holy she understands me. She removes her hands from my shoulders and undoes the clasp but holds her arms to her chest, not letting her bra fall.

I'm desperate.

Too desperate.

Holding her tighter, I bite the cup of her bra and pull the material away. She moans before dropping her hands to her sides, letting the straps fall.

"Fuck," I whisper, cupping both of her phenomenal, bare tits in my hands. Her eyes close—her back arches, pushing her breasts firmer against my palms. I remove a hand and replace it with my mouth. Her fingers grip my hair, her hips slowly thrusting as I kiss her breasts, alternating from one to the other. Licking, sucking, biting gently.

"Holy shit, Ky, you feel so fu—" I grab her ass, cutting her off and causing her to yank at my shirt, trying desperately to remove it. I pull away just long enough to do it for her, and then I go back to my task. *Heaven.* She feels like fucking heaven—in my hands, on my face, in my mouth. My cock throbs, urging for a release. I move my hands to her ass, around her hips to the front of her panties. My fingers dip between her thighs and I growl against her nipple, pulling back slightly so I can focus on the wetness I feel through the lace. I look up at her face, but her head's tilted back, her eyes closed, her lower lip trembling with each exhale. "Fuck, you're beautiful, Maddy."

Her eyes snap open, and she looks down at me. Her tits

are practically bouncing with the strength of her breaths. Her gaze drops to my crotch, where my hardness tents the denim. "Off," she orders.

I do as she says, and once I've kicked off my jeans, I look back up at her. "All of it, Ky."

I shake my head. "You first."

She leans down, taking my bottom lip between her teeth. "Off," she repeats, pushing her tongue against mine. Her hands flatten on my thighs, creeping higher, higher, higher until they land—

"Fuck, Madison."

Her fingers circle my dick through my boxers, and she strokes me once.

"You keep going and I'm going to come before we get started."

Her gaze lifts, peering at me through her lashes before a slow, perfect smile pulls on her lips and she stands straighter. "Fine," she whispers, her thumbs running along the waistband of her panties. "Me first, then."

I cover my hard-on, trying to control it somehow, while she makes a show of pushing her underwear down. I'm panting now, unable to control my breathing.

She pushes further—just an inch. And then she stops, one hand reaching for the lamp.

I grab her wrist, and I shake my head when her eyes meet mine. "No. I want to see you. All of you." I sit up on the bed and move to the middle, pulling on her arm until she joins me. We sit on our knees, almost naked, watching each other and taking in every curve, every dip, every inch of exposed skin. Her fingers press against my stomach, but her eyes stay on mine. I lean down to kiss her waiting lips, and instantly, the room fills with the sounds of our tongues lashing, of our mouths moving and of our moans of pleasure. She moves her hand lower until it brushes against my cock, causing it to twitch in her hand. Her mouth curls against mine as she tugs at my boxers, finally freeing my hardness. The warmth of her hand as it circles my length has my breath catching. Her hand moves slowly, all the way up and then all the way down, pausing for a moment to run her thumb across the tip. "Fuck."

I move a hand down her neck, her chest, slowing a beat to appreciate her perfect tits. Then I continue, lower again, past her stomach, only stopping when I feel the warmth of her sex against my palm. I use my other hand to push her panties down her thighs, reveling in the feeling of her naked pussy in my hand. She moans again, squeezing me tighter while I run a finger between her slit until I find the source of her wetness. Her head falls back, and my mouth instinctively finds her nipple as I press a finger into her.

She moves faster, more determined, and I'm so close to the edge, but like she said—her first.

I try to ignore how she's making me feel and wrap my arm around her waist, holding her in place. Then I remove my finger, replace it with two, all the while circling her clit with my thumb, and she thrusts against my hand. "Aah!"

Her hand works faster. "Fuck, Maddy," I moan through gritted teeth.

"Ky, please don't stop!"

My tongue laps at her nipples, my fingers finding the same rhythm as her thrusts.

"Ky, I'm..."

I close my eyes, trying to hold off.

"Shit... Ky!"

She tightens around my fingers, her body shuddering beneath my touch.

She comes around my fingers.

I come on her stomach.

She kisses me until every last drop's expelled.

We stay silent, our chests rising and falling as we try to catch our breaths. "That was…" she whispers.

"*Breathtaking*," I finish for her.

She laughs and releases me. I do the same. Then she looks down at her stomach and the mess that I've made. "Shower?" she asks. "And then you have to stay the night. You can't give a girl a world-shattering orgasm and just leave."

MADISON

PEOPLE DO CRAZY things when they feel like the clock is ticking too fast, or too slow, or not ticking at all.

17

KY

DR. AROMA SMIRKS, eyeing me while she kicks her foot back and forth. "How's that self-pleasuring going for you?"

I laugh once. "I'm getting a little help in that department, actually."

"Oh yeah?"

"I mean we're not sleeping together, if that's what you're thinking."

"That's not the be-all and end-all of a relationship, though."

"Hey now... I didn't say anything about a relationship."

She smiles. "Well, let me ask you a question then."

"Sure."

"Would it hurt you to lose her?"

I shrug, even though I know the truth. "Maybe," I lie.

Her smile widens. "Maybe it's a good thing—you and her. Maybe it's a start."

"A start to what?"

"To you realizing that your existence isn't worthless—that you have something to lose. And maybe it starts with her, but it doesn't have to end there, Ky. You have a lot to lose. You just don't know it yet."

* * *

YOU KNOW WHAT'S better than waking up in bed with Madison? Nothing. Not a goddamn thing.

She rolls over and lazily throws her arm over my stomach when my alarm goes off. "Make it stop."

I sit up, looking around her dim bedroom for my phone. "Where the hell is my phone?"

"Ignore it."

I finally find the flashing light of my phone in the pocket of my jeans, discarded on the floor from last night. "I need to go train."

She wraps both arms around me now, pulling me back down. "Skip it," she mumbles, her eyes still closed.

I kiss her quickly. "I can't," I tell her, smiling when she grunts in response. "I'll be back in a few hours. Your place or mine?"

She murmurs, her face half smeared into the pillow, "We'll find each other. We always do."

* * *

"SO HERE'S WHAT you need to do," Jax says. I'd called him on the way to the gym because he said he had a plan. "Drop your phone on the table next to his when you get a chance and just accidentally pick up his and go through it."

I laugh. "That's your fucking plan?"

"Dude. I can't get authorization on anything here. The guys in the precinct—they kind of hate me."

That gets my attention. "What do you mean they hate you? Are they causing shit for you?"

"Calm down, *Captain Combative*. I'm a big boy now. I can take care of myself."

The tension leaves my shoulders.

He adds, "It's just that I'm young—the youngest who's ever made detective. And all the old timers—even sarge—they don't want to listen to a punk like me."

"That's... fair, I guess."

"I know DeLuca's there at the moment, and you said you guys had the same phone, so just try it. What harm can it do?"

"He could kick my ass."

"You can take it."

"This is a shit plan, Jax."

"Just *try*. That's all I'm asking."

I STEP INTO the gym and bump fists with Tiny, who's standing next to the door. I eye him up and down. "You're here a lot. Ever think of maybe doing more than just standing at the door?" I tap his stomach with the back of my hand.

He hides his smile.

"Seriously, though," I joke. "You could stand to lose a few."

He runs his hands down his gut, a slow smirk pulling on his lips. "And get rid of the lady magnet?" He releases a chuckle from deep in his throat. "The ladies love it! More bounce per ounce."

I chuckle. "More fun per ton."

He lets out an all-consuming laugh that has his entire body jiggling.

"Yo," I start, then look behind me at DeLuca sitting at his regular table, phone and laptop in front of him. I turn back to Tiny. "You want to grab some burgers after this?"

His eyes widen and he licks his lips.

"Tiny!" DeLuca shouts, and we both face him. He's on his feet now, shaking his head at Tiny. He looks pissed and that makes me happy—because I'm getting to him, right in his head.

"Nah, bro," Tiny says. "Can't mix business with pleasure."

I nod once. "Got it," I say, moving from him to DeLuca. "Sorry, man," I lie. "I didn't mean any disrespect." I glance down at his phone sitting on the table, unlocked and on the home screen. I point to Tiny, hoping his gaze will follow. When it does, I drop my phone next to his. "I'm just trying to entertain him, you know? He seems like a good guy."

DeLuca clears his throat before looking up at me. "He is a good guy. He's also *my* guy."

"Like I said—"

"Yo, Boss Man!" Tiny calls out. "You have a visitor." He jerks his head to a blonde standing by the door.

DeLuca swears under his breath and pushes off the seat before making his way over to her.

Perfect.

I turn my back, blocking them from seeing my his phone now in my hand. I peek over my shoulder—but DeLuca and Blondie are deep in heated whispers.

The home screen on his phone is in another language, so I tap the phone icon and go to recent calls. All the names are numbers, like a code of some kind, and that's as far as I get before I hear DeLuca yell, "Just tell her to fuck off next time!"

I drop the phone back on the table and swiftly make my way to the row of chairs against the back wall. I've just stripped off my shirt when DeLuca speaks from behind me. "A word, Parker?" I turn to him—but his expression, just like his words, is calm.

Too fucking calm.

He jerks his head toward the change room and doesn't wait for my response; he simply leads me to the room. Once we're both in and the door is locked, I'm pinned to the wall, his forearm against my throat. "How fucking stupid do you think I am?"

I try to push him away.

He presses harder, cutting off air to my lungs.

"What the fuck are you talking about?" I stammer.

He doesn't reply, but his punch right to my fucking mouth says it all. I use all my strength to push off the wall and into him, my fist around his shirt, shoving him until his back hits a set of lockers. "Don't fucking touch me again."

He smiles, this sinister fucking smile that does nothing more than build my rage. My free hands form a fist, ready to pay back his assault.

But he's fast.

Too fucking fast.

Again.

I don't even notice him pull the gun from his back, don't even know he has it, until it makes contact with my chin. "Don't. Touch. My. Shit. *Ever.*"

"Fuck you!"

He presses the gun firmer into me.

I hold my ground.

The door bursts open.

"What the fuck!" I'd never seen a fat cunt move so fast. "Let it go, man," Tiny says to DeLuca, pulling him off me.

DeLuca drops his hand and takes a step back, his eyes on mine. "Get the car, Tiny." He looks me up and down with that same fucking calm in his eyes. "I'm done here."

MADISON

Sara: What are you doing?
Madison: Walking.
Sara: On your own?
Sara: You there?

KY

I FIGHT A war in my head, trying to work out what to reveal to Jackson and what to keep to myself. I decide on the facts that are of interest to the case and nothing else. The personal vendetta I have on DeLuca is exactly that—*personal*. I tell him about DeLuca's phone and the numbered codes, and I tell him about it being set to a different language. "What language?" he asks.

I stop and lean against a building on the way home from the gym. "I can't be sure. DeLuca... sounds Italian, right? Maybe it's that."

"Maybe. Thanks for getting that info. Doesn't really help much, though."

"Sorry, man. I'll keep trying."

"It's all we can do. Keep me in the loop on everything."

"Yeah."

"*Everything,* Ky. I mean it."

* * *

MADISON JUMPS UP from the seat in the foyer when I enter the building. I wish it were one of those times when seeing her would make me forget everything else. Unfortunately, it isn't. And I can lie to her... lie to Jax, even. But I can't lie to myself. "Morning, Kyler," she coos, sauntering toward me. She curls her arm around my neck and leans up for a kiss, but she stops halfway, pouting as she runs her thumb across the cut on my lip.

I rear back and push her hand away, taking in her frown as I mumble an apology.

"I take it it wasn't a good session?" she asks.

I swing my gym bag behind me and wrap my arms around her waist. "Sucked. I just wanted to be back in bed with you."

"So you missed me, huh?"

"Always."

She jerks her head toward the mailboxes. "Are you going to you check your mail today?

There might be a surprise... you know... other than bills or credit card applications."

I spin on my heels and move toward the boxes. Over my shoulder I say, "How did you get into my mailbox?"

She follows, stopping next to me as I turn the key. "Frank," she says.

"Who the hell's Frank?"

"Jeez, Ky. You don't know the maintenance guy?"

I shake my head while I open the box, my breath halting when I take sight of the single pink rose.

"Debbie said it was the color for thankfulness."

I pull out the flower and pretend to examine it, but my mind's reeling. "When did you see Debbie?"

"This morning while you were at the gym."

I glance up at her. "You went out on your own?"

She nods proudly. "Yup!"

"By yourself?"

Another nod.

"And your anxiety?"

"Not so bad." She shrugs. "It was worth it. I just wanted to find a way to show you how I feel about you."

"You're thankful?"

"For you, Ky. Yes. I'm thankful."

* * *

SLUMPING DOWN ON the couch, I start to unwrap the tape from around my fingers. Morning sessions at the gym focus on martial arts. Gunner and I spent most of the time sparring in the cage while he taught me different moves: defense and offense. Gunner knows a hell of a lot more about skilled martial arts. Me? I kind of just like to punch things. So far, that's been enough. But if I want to get DeLuca, I need time. Which means that I need to make it through my first fight. So, I need the training. And that means I need Gunner. Still, knowing how to fight in the ring doesn't save me from a fucking bullet through my head.

I need to start carrying.

"I'LL DO IT, babe," Madison says, pulling me from my thoughts. She sits next to me and covers my hands with hers, then carefully flips my hand, palm up, her brow bunching as she inspects it. "Does it hurt?"

"No. It's not injury tape," I say. "It's just precautionary."

Her jaw works as she slowly removes the tape from each finger. I sigh, unable to remember the last time someone's held my hand or has been this gentle with me. I kiss the top of her head, breathing her in.

"What was that for?" she asks, lifting her gaze.

"It just feels good to be cared for, you know?"

She quickly looks away and refocuses on my other hand. "Yeah. I *do* know."

WE GO TO the dollar store and get her another frame. Then we end up having lunch at a random diner Debbie told her about this morning. When I ask for the bill, the waitress tells me that it's taken care of and sets a note on the table in front of me. I manage to read it quickly before Madison reaches over and pulls it from under my nose. "Thank you for your service," she reads out loud.

Looking down at myself, I try to work out how someone would know. I kick myself for not realizing I'm wearing my Army PT shirt. Sighing, I hide my dog tags behind my shirt and look up at the waitress. "Who did this?"

The waitress just shrugs. "They wanted to remain anonymous, but they've already left."

"Thanks."

"No," she says, shaking her head. "Thank you."

* * *

I'M QUIET ON the way home. So is Maddy. I know she wants to say something because she starts a few times, only to stop and drop her gaze. I hold on to her hand tighter so she understands that I'm not upset at her. I'm just upset.

Once we're in her apartment, she orders me to sit on the floor in front of the couch while she sits behind me, her legs wrapped around my torso and her hands massaging my shoulders. I stretch my neck, welcoming her touch. "I needed this," I tell her. My body was starting to feel the effects of the rigorous training and lack of actual rest. When I'm not at the gym, I'm with her, which means a *lot* of walking. The only time I get to sit down is during meals and, clearly, that isn't enough.

"You seemed tense," she says, digging her thumb under my shoulder blade. "Does it happen often?"

"What?"

"People thanking you like that."

"First time for me," I tell her. "But I've heard stories about it."

"And you don't like it?"

I moan when her thumb finds a knot in the middle of my back. "I don't deserve it," I manage to say.

"You can't say that—"

"Yeah, I can," I cut in, leaning forward and away from her touch.

"Why can't you accept someone's gratitude?"

I sit on the couch and pat my lap, and she instantly crawls on her knees until she's sitting on me, straddling my waist. She cups my face, kisses me once, and then pulls back, leaving her hands in place. "What is it, babe?"

I push my head further into her hands.

And then I tell her.

I tell her *everything*.

KY: AGE 17

It was a week exactly since Jeff died and a few days since the funeral... which was also the day I found out my ex-girlfriend was a whore. I was so fucking sick of feeling.

Seventeen years—hundreds of beatings—and I'd never felt as low as I did then. I wanted the pain of a thousand knives effortlessly stabbing my heart to stop. Just for one night. Hell, even for a few hours. So I did something I thought I'd never do.

I called Steve.

We hadn't spoken since the night Jeff died, but if there was anyone that could help me forget, it was my drop-kick of a brother.

He didn't answer. Not the first time and not the ten times after that.

I'd almost given up hope when he called back close to midnight. "I was working. What happened? Are you okay?" he rushed out, genuine concern in his voice. And for a moment, I remembered why I spent so many years admiring him. Because he did genuinely care.

"I'm fine."

"So what's up?"

"I need your help."

"What kind of help, Ky?"

I stayed silent.

On his end, a lighter flicked and he inhaled what was either a joint or a cigarette. "You're after drugs, aren't you?"

"Yes," I whispered, my voice trembling.

"No."

"Why?" I bit out.

"Because, Ky. You're not like that. I'm not going to be responsible for—"

"Come on, Steve. I've never asked you for anything. Ever. Just give me this."

"I can't," he answered, taking another drag of his smoke. "I know what you're feeling right now—I've been there. And I saw you at Jeff's funeral."

"You were there?"

"Exactly, Ky. You had no fucking clue what was going on around you. You think drugs are gonna help?" He laughed once but not out of humor. "Trust me, dude, I get it. How the fuck do you think I turned out the way I did?"

We were both silent for so long that I thought we were done. I'd almost hung up when he sighed loudly. "I kind of have other plans. I didn't want to be doing anything tonight."

"Please, Steve? You know I wouldn't ask..."

He spoke quietly to someone else, then said, "Fine. Meet me at my work. I don't have anything on me, but there's a field party where I can get some. I'll take you there, get some stuff, but then I'm done, okay? I have company."

THERE WAS NO greeting when I pulled into the parking lot at his work. He reversed out of the spot and drove farther out of town. I followed behind, my hands gripping the steering wheel tighter with every passing mile. There was a part of me that was anxious, maybe even afraid. But none of that compared to how badly I needed to forget.

By the time we got to the field, twenty minutes had passed. I waited with my hands shoved in my pockets while he helped his 'company' out of his car, rolling my eyes when I heard him ask her what her name was.

Steve made himself comfortable on the hood of my car, his girl pressed to his side while he ran his hand up and down her arm to warm her. "What are you thinking? Weed? Ecstasy?"

I stood in front of them, looking down at the ground, then I shrugged.

Steve laughed once. "Have you ever taken anything before?"

I was out of my element. I'd always been straight edge. Yeah, I'd drink on weekends, but I was always careful not to cross a certain line. Right now, I wanted that line crossed, and I wanted it far, far behind me. And Steve—he was going to help me do that.

My silence must have been answer enough. One phone call and five minutes later, some guy I'd never seen before started approaching us.

They shook hands, the way I'd seen so many times on TV when they were doing the discreet handover.

"We'll start with weed," Steve said, like it was the most casual thing in the world. He went back in his car, leaving his girl with me.

"Is this weird?" I asked her. She was wearing clothes that seemed way too big on her. The hood of her sweatshirt covered most of her face, and the moonlight wasn't enough to show the rest of it. She shrugged but didn't say a word. Neither did I.

A minute later, he came back with a joint, sparked it, took a drag, and passed it to me.

I lifted the joint to my dry lips, nervously anticipating the effect it would have on me.

I choked.

It was the first time I'd smoked anything, and the harshness of it did immediate damage to my throat.

Steve laughed, patting me on my shoulder. "Take it easy, bro. You're a virgin."

I coughed until my eyes watered, and when I finally recovered, I took another drag, slower and more prepared this time. I offered the joint to his girl, but she politely declined.

"Now what?" I asked as he took it from between my fingers.

"Now we wait."

I'd heard that the major side effect of weed, apart from the high, was the paranoia. It only took ten minutes and one more drag for me to start feeling it full force. Steve didn't even look affected. Or maybe that's just because he was high all the fucking time and I didn't know better. At some point, who knows how long, all three of us ended up lying on the hood of my car looking up at the stars. "I wish I may, I wish I might..." I mumbled.

"Fuck your wish," Steve finished for me.

We both scoffed.

"Are you feeling it yet?" he asked.

"Feeling what?"

He didn't answer right away. "Better. Did it work for you? Are you forgetting the pain?" His voice was low, almost distant.

I turned to him, but his eyes were closed. I tried to answer his question... Did it work? I thought about Jeff and Ashlee, and I thought about Christine and Jax... then I felt something wet streaming down my cheek. Fuck, I was crying. I quickly wiped my tears, hoping Steve hadn't seen it. "It didn't, did it?" he said, but it wasn't a question. "It doesn't take the pain away. Sometimes, it even amplifies it." He sighed, finally opening his eyes and turning to me. "I used to be you. At first, that's why I did it... but it didn't take anything away. That pain you feel, it's inside you. It thrives, lives, and breathes in your head. Nothing can take that away from you..." Then he laughed—which sounded so off considering his words. "Kyler... I'm going to say this once, and then we're going to forget I ever said it. You—you're kind of amazing. The way you haven't let it get to you like it did me. I'm glad you have Jax and his family, man. But I have a feeling even if they weren't there, you'd still find a way to turn it all around, you know?"

His words had my head spinning.

Or maybe the car was spinning.

Fuck it. Maybe the entire world was spinning.

He added, "You remember what I said the day I told you I was leaving?" He didn't wait for my response. "You said, 'You shouldn't let 'em take it.' I asked you what the hell you were talking about it. You said, 'You, Steve, don't let them own you.'" He raised his hand and wiped at his cheek. "But here I am, Ky, letting them take me. And you know why? Because that pain I feel, it's inside me. Just like it's inside you, and no amount of drugs can change that." He brought up the girl's hand he was holding and kissed the back of it. "Go home, Ky. Go home to your family..." He waved his finger in a circle, "... and be better than this. You don't belong here." It wasn't said out of anger or bitterness. It seemed like he was resigned to the fact that this was his life and, at that moment, I could tell he fucking hated it.

"You don't have to belong here either, Steve."

He let out a bitter laugh. "A little late for all that." He got off the hood and helped his girl down and then offered me his hand.

To say that I felt like ass was an understatement.

"Are you good to drive?" he asked, helping me into my car.

I told him I was fine.

I wasn't.

He nodded as he lit up a smoke. "I love you, bro. Take care, all right?"

I returned his nod, started the car, and peeled out of there.

I got about two miles down the road before I pulled over and puked. Fuck weed. And fuck Steve. Because he was right; it didn't help at all.

When I stumbled back in the car, I could barely move, let alone drive.

So I slept.

The sound of sirens startled me awake. My eyes tried to focus on the dozen cop cars and ambulances speeding past me, and my full-blown paranoia took over. I got out of there as fast as possible, doing everything I could to keep my focus on the roads. I don't even remember how I managed to get home, but I sure as hell remember what happened next.

IT FELT LIKE the entire house was shaking with the constant banging on the door.

"Kyler!" a man shouted, and the banging started again.

My pulse sped. It could only be one man—my dad.

I shrugged on a shirt and ran downstairs, ignoring the fog in my head from the weed the night before. Christine was already at the door, peeking out the window next to it. She was prepared this time, shotgun in hand. "What do you want?" she yelled.

"I need to speak to Ky!"

Jackson stood beside me just as Christine turned to me. "You say the word and I'll order him to leave."

I squared my shoulders, took a step forward and opened the door, ready to come face-to-face with the devil.

With Jax behind and me, and Christine was right next to him, my voice broke when I said, "What do you want?"

The devil's gaze flicked from Jackson to Christine and then settled on me. His face was red but not out of anger. He wiped his eyes, and I saw it then—a completely different side of him. "It's your brother," he said quietly.

And even though I already knew the answer—still, I found myself asking, "What about him?"

"He's dead, Ky."

* * *

THE OFFICIAL CAUSE of death was a drug overdose. The unofficial cause was that he'd taken bad drugs. Word was that it was bad ecstasy laced with crack. Whatever the fuck it was—it had killed him. And I was one of the last people to see him. I was also the reason he was there in the first place. I asked him—no—I begged him to go. And now he was dead.

Just like Jeff.

THE FUNERAL WAS small. The party next door wasn't.

I didn't know what to do. I could barely function. I'd held in my tears when Jeff died, but it felt like I'd lost everything important to me. And as much as Christine and Jax tried to comfort me, I felt completely alone. And that was my fault. I isolated myself from them because I couldn't deal and I didn't want my burden on them.

They'd already been through enough.

But the worst part was the guilt.

It was overwhelming.

So was the pain.

So was the anger.

I was so fucking angry.

"It's okay to show your suffering, Kyler," Christine said, stepping into my room and placing a tray of food on my nightstand. "You've

lost two people very dear to you. Two people you loved... all in a week. It's okay to feel sorry for yourself."

It wasn't okay.

She had no fucking clue what she was talking about because I didn't deserve to feel anything but pain. I got out of bed and held the door open for her. "Get out."

"Kyler!"

"Get out!"

Jackson stepped out of his room and into the hallway. "Don't talk to Mom like that!"

"It's fine, Jackson," Christine said, but she was looking right at me. "It's fine," she repeated, the tears caused by disappointment replacing the sadness and pity.

"It is fine," I said, staring down at her. "You're allowed to hate me. I hate me, too."

* * *

Two days later I turned eighteen and walked into the army recruiter's office.

Three months later, I graduated.

That night, I packed my bags and slipped a note under Jackson's bedroom door. I told him to take care of his mom. I apologized for not being able to be the man they expected—the man I wanted to be.

And I told him that I loved them both.

Then I got on a bus to Ft. Hood, Texas.

And I never looked back.

MADISON

Ky's story plays out in mind like a vivid movie.

Because it's more than just his memories...

It's mine, too.

Shit.

KY

SHE BLOWS OUT a heavy breath, my name coming out with it.

I turn away, not wanting to see the pity in her eyes. "So, no, Madison, I don't think I deserve people's gratitude. People enlist for honorable reasons. I enlisted because I wanted an out."

"That doesn't mean—"

"It means *everything*," I cut in, the frustration in my voice evident. I take a calming breath and try to end the conversation. "That's all of me, Maddy."

"So Ashlee..." she trails off.

I look back at her.

"She's the reason you haven't *been* with anyone since you were seventeen?"

My eyebrows pinch. "What?"

"You said that—"

I grimace. "No. I think you misunderstood." I tread carefully. "I said I hadn't *dated* since I was seventeen. That doesn't mean I haven't been with anyone—"

"Oh!" Her eyes go huge, then she scrunches her nose in disgust. She tries to get off my lap, but I hold on to her tighter.

"I just want to be honest with you, Madison. And now that you know about Ashlee and what she did—the hurt she caused—I expect you to do the same. I don't like vague, and I don't want secrets between us. I don't want to feel like that again."

Her gaze drops between us, and she doesn't respond—not with words, and not with anything else. She scoots back, trying to remove herself from my hold, and I let her this time. She looks at the clock and says, "It's time for you to leave."

I pull on her dress until she's between my legs. "You're mad?"

She shakes her head.

"You can't be mad. I could've lied to you."

"I know," she says, her hands in my hair, causing my eyes to drift shut at her touch. "I just feel less... I don't know. You tell me that you've been with girls that probably mean nothing to you, and now I'm scared that maybe I'm one of them."

"Don't do that."

"What?"

"Sell yourself short. You're pretty much the only thing that means anything to me."

She leans down, resting her forehead on mine. "Promise?"

"Promise."

She kisses me softly, her lips curving into a smile. "Good," she says, right before her tongue sweeps across mine. We kiss for nowhere near long enough before I have to pull away. "I have to go."

"No!" She exaggerates one of her infamous pouts. "Skip it."

"I can't." I grab my phone off the coffee table and check the time, knowing I'm already late.

"Why not?" she whines.

"Because I *have* to go."

"That's not a good enough excuse."

"Come with me," I say, before I can think straight. I walk over to the kitchen counter and grab my iPad. "You can use this. It'll make time go faster."

* * *

GUNNER'S EYES WIDEN when he sees Madison walk in behind

me, but the reaction's short-lived and he goes back to the Gunner I know. "You're late, Parker!"

"I was busy."

He looks Madison up and down, more than once, and I ball my fists at my sides to keep my jealousy in check. The last thing I need is another unexpected brawl.

I lead Madison to a chair against the back wall and connect the iPad to the gym Wi-Fi before handing it to her. "I'll be done soon." I make sure Gunner's watching when I lean in to give her a kiss... a nice, long, *possessive* kiss.

She rolls her eyes when we pull apart, her gaze darting behind me to where I assume Gunner's standing. Then she smirks, pulls me down by my shirt and gives me an even longer, even sexier kiss. I chuckle into her mouth before she pulls away. "Good luck," she whispers, and I shake my head, laughing as I make my way over to the weights.

"Well, well, well," I hear and stop in my tracks. I quickly face DeLuca, but he's already sitting next to Madison, whose face has paled completely. She sits up straighter, her shoulders rigid. "Maybe it's time I watch you in action," DeLuca says, leaning back in his chair and throwing an arm behind Madison.

I make my way over to Madison and do my best to ignore DeLuca's presence. "You good, babe?"

She nods quickly. "Yeah. You go ahead. I'll..." She lifts the iPad and smiles.

"Let's spar!" Gunner yells. I back away, my gaze flicking between the two of them. DeLuca doesn't budge. He doesn't show a single emotion.

I hate it.

I hate *him*.

I turn to Gunner. "We sparred this morning. I thought we were doing strength and conditioning?"

"Is this your gym?" he spits out. "I didn't think so."

"Whatever you say, man." I head back over to Maddy, where my gear is.

"No gloves. No gear!" he yells.

I rest my hands on my hips and shake my head. *Fuck him.* I strip off my shirt and throw it at Madison.

When I get in the cage, Gunner's eyes skim over my ribs, inspecting the remnants of the damage he'd helped create the week before.

I try to concentrate because I want DeLuca to see that I'm not just some chump in the cage. I want him to know that I'm learning—and that I'm *good*—so that if he ever feels the need to attack me again, I'll be more than ready to fight back.

After an hour of sparring and Gunner 'talking' me through it, he says he wants to show me one more move before taking a break. I'm beat, but my conditioning is good. I train hard every day, pushing myself to my absolute limit. Gunner—he's fucked. He can barely speak, from both his lack of oxygen and the sweat covering his entire face.

He glances over at DeLuca for a second, but it's long enough for me to follow his gaze—and long enough for me to see DeLuca jerk his head once. He gets up from beside Madison, taps her once on the shoulder, and leaves the building.

"Focus," Gunner clips. "You need to work on your sprawl. Your balance is off." My attention now on him, I nod in agreement. Sprawling isn't my greatest skill. "I'm going to go for a single leg takedown," he says.

"Okay." I set my feet apart, plant them to the floor and bend my knees, giving myself maximum defensive resistance. The plan is that he'll move forward—try to take me down by grabbing one of my legs. If it works out for him, I'll be on the ground. If it works for me, I'll be able to scoot my legs back quick enough that I'd land on his upper back and gain an advantage.

But he doesn't go for the takedown.

He goes straight for my ribs... with his goddamn shoulder.

I fly back, all air leaving my lungs while flashes of white hit the backs of my eyes. Somewhere in the distance, I hear Madison scream. I wince, rolling to my left and nursing my right ribcage.

"What the fuck is wrong with you, you asshole!" Madison yells. I hear the cage door open and slam shut and the next moment... tits ...all up in my vision.

Maybe I'm dreaming.

"Ky! Are you okay?"

"Yeah." I try to move, but the pain's too overwhelming.

She's on her knees, her hand stroking my forehead. Then, suddenly, rage fills her eyes and her face turns red. "You did that on purpose, you dick!" she yells at Gunner. Then to me, "Can you sit up?"

I shake my head. I can get up, but I like my view just fine.

She runs her hands through my hair and lifts my head off the mat, holding me to her. I smile against her chest. "Are you hurt?" she asks.

"Yeah." I exaggerate a groan. "Oh, man. It hurts so damn bad."

She pulls away, her eyes narrowed. "Are you fucking with me?"

I laugh, which reminds me of the true physical pain I'm in. "No," I lie. I reach out and grab her arm, trying to bring her back to me. "Come back and comfort me—that made me feel a *whole* lot better."

She glares at me but helps me stand, then turns to Gunner. "You're an asshole, *Gunther*."

My laugh's cut short by my wince. My ribs aren't broken, but they're pretty damn close. She helps me with my shirt and walks me out of the gym.

* * *

"What the hell's his problem?" she asks, stopping in front of the dollar store. "I bet he has a tiny dick."

I laugh and then almost cry out in my pain. "Fuck. Don't make me laugh."

"And you!" She pokes a finger into my shoulder. "I was so worried you broke something and you—"

I raise my hand, cutting her off. "I'm not going to apologize for being a guy. Don't expect it."

She rears back and gives me that same disgusted look all girls give to idiot jack-holes. "I'll be back," she says, walking into the store.

I lean against the wall and quit faking for a moment.

I hurt.

Bad.

And I need time to recover.

I pull out my phone and send a text to Jackson.

Ky: *I can't train for a few days.*
Jackson: *You okay?*
Ky: *Yeah, my ribs copped a beating.*
Jackson: *How?*
Ky: *Not important.*

* * *

Madison helps me to the couch and, not a minute later, there's a knock on the door. "Are you expecting someone?"

"Nope."

She opens the door to Jackson's surprised face. They both turn to me, and Jackson says, "How bad is it?"

"He already knows?" Madison asks, confusion clear in her tone.

"Yeah," Jackson answers after a momentary panic. "He asked for a recommendation for a doctor to check it out."

Madison's eyes widen. "It's that bad?"

They both stalk toward me as if I'm an injured animal they need to assess. "Just precautionary." I glare at Jackson. "I'm fine."

"I'll get the ice," Madison says, making her way to the kitchen.

Jax sits next to me and kicks his legs up on the coffee table. "Playing house already. You've known her how long? A few days?"

"Leave it alone, Jax."

"How much do you know about her?"

"Enough."

Madison returns with an ice pack and sits on my other side. She lifts my shirt, completely ignoring the fact that Jackson is watching her intently. "It's not looking so good," she says, placing the pack on my right side.

I flinch.

She cringes. "We'll stay in. I'll get some menus." She looks up at Jackson. "Did you want to stay for dinner?"

He shakes his head. "I have a little work to do. Was just checking in on my big bro."

She nods as she stands up and, once she's in the kitchen, far enough that she can't hear us, Jax laughs. "Is she going for some bride speed record?"

"Are you jealous?"

"I'm serious, bro." And the look on his face lets me know it. "Do you even know her last name?"

"Why?" I ask, incredulously. "Are you going to do a background check?"

He rolls his eyes.

"Maddy!" I shout, my eyes on Jax.

"Yeah?"

"What's your last name?"

"Haynes."

I raise my eyebrows at Jackson.

"Why?" she says, coming back over with a bunch of take-out menus.

I shrug. "Just realized I didn't know it."

She smiles awkwardly, her eyes flicking to Jackson before attempting to look busy with the menus.

"So, a few days?" Jax asks.

"At least three, I'd say."

"Okay. I'll text you the number for my doctor. Get him to check it out." Standing up, he adds, "Madison, good seeing you again." She smiles at him, still awkward. "I'll let myself out."

Once he's out, Madison says, the sadness in her tone unmistakable, "He hates me."

"No, he doesn't."

"Yeah, he does."

"He's just protective."

"Of a girl?" she laughs.

I shrug. "History."

* * *

"I'M SO FULL." Madison leans back on the couch after finishing dinner and pats her stomach twice. "I'm kind of happy you got the next few days off. It means we can hang out more."

"I didn't really plan on spending all that time off with *you,*" I joke, earning a backhand to the stomach. The pain in my ribs is instant, and I wince out a "Fuck."

Madison faces me, her eyes wide. "Shit, Ky. I'm so sorry. I forgot."

I hold my breath and let the ache filter out of me. Her

gaze focuses on my ribs, a perfect frown pulling on her lips while she attempts to fight back tears. "Maddy, it's fine. It was an accident."

She stands. "I should go."

I grab her arm. "No. Stay with me tonight."

"I'll just hurt you more."

"No, you won't. Stop being dramatic. Plus, what if I need your help to pee in the middle of the night? Do you really want to be the reason I wet the bed?"

It's supposed to be a joke, but she isn't laughing. "It's that bad?"

"Yeah. *Really* bad." I fake a grimace. "Please, Maddy, it hurts *so* damn much."

She narrows her eyes at me while I try to contain my laugh. "You could just ask, you know." She leans down and kisses me quickly. "I'll just grab some things and be right back."

* * *

AN HOUR LATER, she's sitting on my bed looking down at me, her finger gently tracing the dips in my stomach. "What's war like?"

I rest my hands behind my head, savoring her touch. "What do you want to know?"

"Do you think it changed you? The experience, I mean."

"Definitely."

"How?"

I reach for her hand and kiss her wrist, then rest it on my chest. "I don't know. When I left, I was just pissed off at the world. I thought I'd learned enough during boot camp, but it was nothing compared to actually being there. You see some bad shit—shit no one should ever have to see—but I think the biggest thing that changed me was meeting my brothers."

"Jackson and Steven?"

"No, I mean my squad brothers. They all had different reasons for enlisting. My buddy Hunter—he lost his dad in 9/11. Montoya—he enlisted to honor his family. Generations of men in his family were soldiers. You'd think that the pressure would suck, but he didn't hate it like I probably would have. He was proud. I mean, they were all proud to be there, you know? Me? I was there because I felt sorry for myself. Because I wanted to run away from reality—a reality that wasn't all that bad—not compared to war."

"Do you regret it though?"

"Not for a second." I don't skip a beat. "Do I regret my reason for joining? Yes. But I wouldn't take it back."

"Is that part of the reason you won't see Christine?"

I inhale a sharp breath, ignoring the discomfort in my ribs. "She didn't know I was enlisting, Maddy. I never told her or Jax. I packed my shit in the middle of the night and left them a note." A bitter laugh bubbles out of me. "A stupid note. Like it would make up for my actions. Truthfully, I'm too embarrassed to face her."

"You think she'd still care about that? I'm sure she'd just want to see you—know that you're alive and well."

"Maybe," I tell her. "But that doesn't take away the shame."

A sad smile forms on her lips before she moves under the covers and rests her head on my shoulder. "Ky?"

"Yeah?"

"Do you think you'll go back? Re-deploy?"

I let my thoughts form into words, and then I tell her the truth. "It used to be my plan. I didn't think there was anything here worth staying for."

"And now?"

I tilt her head up and kiss her once, letting my lips linger. "And now I have you, Maddy."

"You have me," she repeats, smiling against my lips. "Will you tell me about her?" she asks, pulling away.

"Who?"

"Christine."

I stare up at the ceiling—memories of Christine filling my mind. "She's badass."

"*Badass?*"

"Yeah. She grew up on this farm—was raised by her dad—kind of reminds me of you, actually."

"Me?"

"Yeah. She's super sweet... seems super innocent. Bakes cookies and crafts and stuff, but then she has this badass side to her. Like, she knows how to carry a gun and isn't afraid to use it."

"I hate guns."

Her words surprise me. "Why?"

"Never mind."

"You avoid talking about anything related to you. You do it all the time. Or you change the subject. You don't think I notice, but I do."

She turns to her side, facing away from me. "Good night, Ky."

"Really? You're just going to act oblivious to it all?"

She starts to shuffle out of bed. "I'm going home."

"No." I ignore the shooting pain and reach over to her, bringing her back down. "Just stay. Forget I said anything."

Her eyes lock on mine when she turns around. "We both have secrets, Ky," she says through a sigh, getting back into bed and facing the ceiling.

"What are you talking about?" I ask, frustration clear in my tone. "You ask a million questions and I answer all of them."

She sighs loudly, resting her head back on my shoulder, and I calm myself down, feeling the tension in my muscles slowly releasing. "It's been a shitty day, Ky," she says. "We should get some sleep before we both say or do something stupid. We'll forget about all of this in the morning."

MADISON

I SAW THE hurt in his eyes, and I almost told him everything.
Almost.
But then... where the hell would I even start?

19

KY

"KY."

I slap the hand away from my face.

"Ky!"

I groan and grab Madison's hand when her finger pokes at my cheek. Her smile's the first thing I see when I open my eyes. "What do you want, Maddy?"

The smile turns to a pout.

"Don't pout. It's annoying," I lie.

Her face falls. "I'm annoying?" She reaches up with her free hand to poke my face again.

I push her hand away. "Yes. *You're* annoying."

She pouts again.

I roll my eyes.

"I just wanted to feel how deep your dimples are," she murmurs. "Are you still mad at me?"

"No. I'm mad at myself because I should be mad at you, but I can't be. And I'm frustrated because I want to kiss you so bad right now, but you don't deserve it."

"Ky?"

"Mm?"

She leans over me, her gaze flicking between my lips to my eyes and back again, right before she presses her lips to mine.

"You're evil," I tell her.

She doesn't skip a beat, just kisses me again. Once. Twice. And by the third time, I've already given in to her. When she pulls away, I say, "Another one."

She laughs. "With pleasure."

* * *

ONCE WE'VE FINISHED eating breakfast and she's cleaned up after us, she grabs the frame she bought yesterday and sits on the couch next to me. Making sure not to hurt my ribs, she leans into my side and rests her hand on my chest. "What do you think their story is?" she asks.

I look at the picture in the frame. The couple's younger than the last. They're on the dock at a lake—the girl's sitting across the guy's lap, and they're holding each other, smiling, like the world's never shown them an ounce of tragedy or regret.

"High school sweethearts," I mumble. "For sure."

From the corner of my eye, I see her watching me, but I keep my gaze on the picture.

"You think?" she asks.

I nod. "You can see it in their smiles. Reality hasn't kicked their asses yet."

She shifts beside me. "She looks like Ashlee."

My eyes snap to hers. "How do you—"

"I—I was on—on your iPad yesterday and I clicked on this blue thing with the letter F—"

I raised my voice. "You went on my Facebook?"

She shrugs. "I guess that could be it."

"Why the hell would you do that?"

"I—I didn't know what it was. I just clicked it."

"So you decided to go through my shit?"

She ignores my question. "There are pictures of you together..."

"Yeah. From five or six years ago. Did you see that? And it doesn't matter, because that shit's personal, Maddy. You shouldn't be going—"

"I didn't know what it was!"

I inhale sharply, pushing down the pain and trying to keep my anger in check. I'm pissed—at her for doing what she did —and because... "You know what? After last night, I thought I'd be okay with it. I've always been honest with you. You ask and I answer. That's how this works. But it's not enough, is it? You had to go through my stuff!"

"Ky—"

"No, Maddy. You know everything about me. I've laid it all out for you. Everything. And after the shit with Ashlee— the hurt she fucking caused me—you should know that I wouldn't deal with secrets and I shouldn't fucking have to."

"I'm the one with secrets?" she yells. "She messaged you *two* days ago, Ky."

"Jesus Christ, Maddy, you went through my messages?"

She flinches, then narrows her eyes at me. "So what if I did! Don't get all high and mighty and act like you're better than me when you're talking to your ex!"

I stand up, pulling at my hair in frustration, and glare down at her. "You honestly think that I'd do whatever it is you're suggesting? I've been all about you, Madison. Ever since the first day I fucking saw you."

"So why are you talking to her?" she yells.

I start pacing, her gaze following me from her spot on the couch. I take a breath, and then another, before finally admitting the truth. "Because it feels good, okay?" So does saying it out loud, apparently. "It feels nice to have her talk to me—to have her apologize and want me back and for me to be able to tell her to fuck off because I *thought* I'd found someone better."

Her gaze lowers.

It just makes me more pissed. "I don't even know how to feel right now. You're mad for whatever reason, and I'm supposed to feel bad when you're the one who avoids anything personal." I don't even know if it's the fact that she went through my stuff or the fact that we're talking about Ashlee or the unresolved argument we had last night. But whatever it is, I keep going, keep pushing for her to fight back. "You don't tell me anything about yourself or your past. I know fuck all about you. You say you're from around here, but then you tell me you don't know the area that well..."

She visibly swallows.

I add, "What were you like in high school, Madison? Did you date? Did you have boys falling at your feet? Oh, I bet you were so damn sweet and innocent, you didn't know you had guys after you. Yeah..." I release a bitter laugh, nodding with it. "I bet you were *that* girl." I pause, watching her eyes turn to stone. "Do you have brothers and sisters? What are your parents like? How did you lose your virginity—"

"Stop it," she bites out, her teeth clenched.

I stop pacing and face her. "Okay, so I guess all of those questions are off limits." I tap my finger on my chin. "Let's go with something easy then. How about... what high school did you go to?"

Her face turns red, lips pressed tight as she tries to contain her sob. Her eyes fill with tears, but she doesn't let them fall. "Stop it, Ky. Please." She's begging now.

And I almost cave.

Almost give in to her.

Again.

"No, Maddy, I'm not going—"

She stands up, picking up the frames and holding them to her chest before pinning me with her glare.

And my heart stops.

I've seen that same look too many times before.

From Jackson.

From Christine.

Yeah, she's pissed.

But beyond that, she's *disappointed*.

She opens her mouth, but nothing comes out. She makes her way to the door while I sit down on the coffee table, my elbows resting on my knees and my head lowered. I hear the door click.

"Madison," I grind out.

"What, Ky?"

I don't look up. "If you walk out right now because you're too damn scared to open up to me, then don't bother coming back." I sniff, trying to keep it together. "I'm done chasing you."

20

KY

"Do you think these sessions help you at all?" Dr. Aroma asks.

"No."

"Yet you keep coming back."

I sit up straighter. "Do I have a choice?"

She flips open a folder—my file—and skims the pages. "Oh yeah," she sings. "You *have* to be here."

I sigh and roll my eyes at the same time. "Trust you to get my hopes up over nothing."

"Do you?"

"Do I what?" I ask, the irritation in my voice evident.

She doesn't skip a beat. "Do you trust me?"

"No."

"Do you trust anyone?"

I press my lips tighter.

"Do you think you have trust issues?"

"Shouldn't you be the judge of that? I've been sitting here for how many sessions now and you're still asking me things that *you* should be working out."

"You don't give off much, Ky."

"Maybe that's my choice."

"So you *choose* to be closed off and not trust anyone?"

Tapping my foot impatiently, I shrug and look out her window.

"Sucks for anyone who tries to get close to you, Ky. Especially if they love you. Or plan on loving you one of these days."

"Are you talking about Madison?"

"Maybe. Or maybe I'm talking about a certain detective that feels your pain enough to *make* you talk to someone about it."

"So I *don't* I have to be here?"

"I didn't say that. Time's up."

* * *

YOU KNOW WHAT sucks? Being mad at the world and not having an outlet. I'm too injured to train and too pissed at myself to care.

I sleep on the couch, or attempt to anyway. I don't want to miss it when those three knocks sound at my door. The quiet, timid knocks that let me know Madison's on the other side. I've imagined it so many times—the way she'd look when I opened the door—her smile always shy, like she wasn't expecting me to be on the other side, happily accepting her company. I even got up occasionally to peek through the peephole, eying the hallway, hoping she'd be there.

For two days, I didn't leave my apartment, just wishing to God I'd hear that sound.

Knock.

Knock.

Knock.

Nothing.

It never came. And by the third day of nothing, I'd given up hope.

I should've just taken the two steps from my apartment to hers and been the one to deliver the knocks, but that would mean *me* giving in to *her* again.

I gave her an opening, and I gave her an out.

She chose the out.

And the worst part? She left me thinking about Ashlee, the girl I held on such a high pedestal. Just like I did with Madison. Maybe it was my fault—the way I let girls treat me.

What Ashlee and I had—I *thought* was easy. There was no effort in being together. We didn't fuck with each other's heads. Maybe that was the reason she decided to fuck some other guy—but, until that happened, I thought we were perfect.

When Madison and I were together—we were far, *far* from perfect.

We weren't even really that *good*.

Or at least that's what I kept telling myself. It was the only way I could be convinced she wasn't worth it.

I'm still convincing myself of her worth a good half hour after I'd hung up with Debbie from the flower shop. She told me *The Madison* was ready to collect and that she couldn't wait to see *us*. I didn't have the heart to tell her. What was I going to say? It was over before it even began? We just didn't work well together? *She checked my Facebook?* I scoff at myself, then finally collect my balls and the remainder of my courage and knock on her damn door.

After a moment, the knob turns and she opens it, just enough to peek out.

I square my shoulders. "Hi."

"Hi," she squeaks, opening the door wider. She stands a little taller, with her hair a mess, eyes red, and cheeks wet. It's obvious she'd been crying.

For a second, I lose the ability to speak.

To think.

To breathe.

"Ky?" It's one word. My name. But it holds a hundred different meanings. A thousand different questions. She opens the door fully and stands in front of me, her gaze penetrating mine. "Did you need something?"

I force myself to look anywhere but at her. "Debbie called," I tell her, my focus on the inside of her apartment. "She said the—" I stop myself from saying *The Madison*. I don't want to say her name, regardless of what it means. "The Rainbow Rose is ready to collect, and she wanted us to pop in and see her."

"Okay... do you want to? I can go on my own. Or you can just go. It *is* yours."

With a sigh, I let my eyes drift shut. My heart—it's hurting. And the lack of confidence in her words causes the pain. When I open my eyes, she's looking down at the floor. "We should go together. She said she wanted to see *us*."

She nods but doesn't look up. "Give me two minutes to get ready."

"I'll wait downstairs."

WHEN I GET down to the foyer, the first things I see are the mailboxes. A bitter laugh bubbles out of me. *I'll never look at mailboxes the same*. I shove my hand in my pocket and pull out my keys, realizing I haven't checked it in three days.

I open the mailbox and all the air leaves me—just like it did the first day I saw her.

I reach inside and pull out the single blue rose. It had wilted, either from lack of air in its confines or the time it had been there—either way, it was *dead*.

I try to recall if Debbie had mentioned the meaning

behind a blue one, and I can't for the life of me remember. I shove the flower back in and shut the box, then I pull out my phone and search the meaning: *the impossible or the unattainable.*

Before I have a chance to think, the elevator doors open and she steps out—her eyes still lowered. She's wearing a yellow dress that goes down to her knees and a blue sweater. I wonder for a moment if it's a sign. Yellow for friendship, blue for impossible. *An impossible friendship?*

Yup. Pretty much sums up what we are.

MADISON DOESN'T PUT her hand on the crook of my elbow. We don't even touch or speak the entire walk to Debbie's Flowers.

I have nothing to say, or maybe I have too much.

Debbie smiles when we walk in, but her smile fades quickly, her gaze moving first to me and then to Madison. "Come out back, sweetheart. Let's have a look at your flower."

Madison follows behind her as I stand at the front of the store, hands in my pockets, wondering what the hell I'm even doing here.

"Did you give it to him?" I hear Debbie ask.

I can't hear Madison's response or anything after that.

They come back a few minutes later, Madison holding the plant with both hands. She sets it on the counter and reaches into her bag for an envelope filled with cash. "How much do I owe you?" she asks quietly.

"Oh, it's already taken care of," Debbie says.

I clear my throat from behind Madison, and when she turns, she refuses to look at me. "I don't feel comfortable with you paying—"

"It's nothing."

"No. It's *always* something, Ky. Nothing in this world comes for *nothing*."

"I don't want your money."

She turns back around and speaks to Debbie. "I don't want him paying for it. Can I just pay and you give him his money back?"

Debbie shakes her head. "Tell you what... how about you work it off? A couple shifts a week? I could use the help."

"Okay," Madison says with a shrug, dropping the envelope in her bag and picking up the plant.

Once we've left the store, she grabs my arm to stop me. "You go ahead," she says, still unable to look at me. "I'm going to walk around for a bit. Thank you, Ky."

It takes everything in me to not say her name, to not ask her to look at me, to not hold her and apologize for something I wasn't truly sorry for.

Instead, I nod and I quickly walk away.

* * *

I'VE ALMOST FALLEN asleep on the couch when I hear it.

Knock.

Knock.

Knock.

My eyes snap open and I jump to my feet.

Then I wait.

Knock.

Knock.

Knock.

I swing the door open.

Madison stands on the other side, her head lowered and her hands balled at her sides. Then she looks up and inhales deeply. "My mom left my dad and me when I was seven. She found another guy. Another family. A better one. She never contacted me afterward. She just *left*. My dad—he took it badly. He turned to booze and neglect. For years it was *bad*. He never hurt me. He just never cared. And then it got worse because he started taking drugs. It started with marijuana and then stronger stuff. I was surrounded by it. I'd go days without seeing him and—"

"Madison," I cut in. I don't know where this is going, but I'm not sure how much more I can hear.

"Shut up, Ky. Just let me talk."

I swallow the lump in my throat and nod, unable to speak.

Her fingers flex and ball into fists again while a single tear streams down her cheek. "Then he met a woman who took him on a whirlwind of junkie adventures. She was always at the house. She never bothered to learn my name. She called me *'girl'* and treated me like a slave, and my dad never did anything to stop it. After a while she got physical with me. It got to the point I was too afraid to leave my room, only coming out to eat and go to school. Then by the time I got to junior high, I wasn't even enrolled anymore. My dad—I think he just forgot I existed."

My heart beats out of my chest and falls at her feet.

She quickly wipes at her tears. "Then one day, when I was fifteen, I came out for food and found a fifty dollar bill on the kitchen counter. There was no note, no message, no *goodbye.*" She lets out another sob and tries to recover quickly, but her breaths are shaky, causing a strain on her words. "They just left me there," she weeps. "And a part of me was grateful. But fifty dollars doesn't allow you to pay the rent."

"Jesus Christ..."

"So, no, Ky." She finally sees me through tear-filled eyes. "I can't answer your questions about what high school was like for me because I didn't experience it."

"So how—"

"And that's all I can give you right now. And I'm sorry that

I couldn't give it to you earlier. And I'm sorry if it's not enough—"

"Enough?"

"I'm sorry if it's not enough to make you want to talk to me again. Because I've been miserable, Ky. For the last three days I've been sitting in my apartment miserable, and *all* I've wanted is for you to knock on my door and talk to me. I wanted you to understand, but I couldn't talk about it. You gave me a chance, and I just couldn't. And then you shut me out, and you left me *devastated*. And I'm sorry, okay? I'm so sorry."

I reach out and bring her to me.

"I'm sorry that I—"

"No, Madison. *I'm* sorry." I kiss the top of her head and hold her tighter. "I'm sorry that I pushed you. I had no idea..."

She wipes her face on my shirt and looks up at me. "Will you please just talk to me now? Because I *need* you. I know it's wrong for me to *need* you. And I know that you—"

I pull her into my apartment and shut the door behind her. "Fuck, Maddy, you have no idea how fucking sorry I am."

"I don't need you to be sorry. I just need you to talk to me again." I sit us down on the couch and pull her legs over mine. She sniffs away her tears. "I'm sorry I went on your face thing. I honestly—"

"I don't even care anymore." I shake my head. How someone like her is still standing, still appreciating the world the way she does, I have no idea. But just like her outlook on life, she deserves to be cherished.

And I'm going to be the one to cherish her.

"But I—" she starts.

"Shush."

"It's just—"

I kiss her, not just to shut her up, but because I *have* to.

And as I kiss away the taste of tears from her lips, the desperation in our hearts—it finally dawns on me—I *need* her, too.

Fuck her secrets.

Fuck her past.

I'm going to change all of it.

MADISON

WITH EVERY SINGLE kiss, he stole my breath and made it his, holding it captive.

And I knew it then—that whatever we were meant to be, for however long time would allow it, it was going to be breathtakingly, heartbreakingly beautiful.

21

KY

"Can I ask you a question, Doc?"

"Sure," Dr. Aroma says, straightening her shoulders.

"Do you believe in fate?"

She tilts her head slightly, eyeing me with a look of concern. "What do you mean exactly?"

"I mean, do you believe that things happen for a reason?"

"Something specific you want to mention?"

I shrug. "Say, hypothetically of course, that you're in Afghanistan, and you know your time's almost up. Your commander calls you and another guy from your unit in for a chat. He tells you that one of you can go home and it's up to you two to decide. You and the other guy draw straws. You win, but you have nothing waiting for you at home. The guy that ends up staying back has a wife who's pregnant. Still, you picked the longer straw, so you go home... to nothing. Two weeks later, the other guy gets shot in an ambush while on patrol. He dies. All the while, you're sitting alone in your apartment feeling sorry for yourself until the day you go to his funeral."

"Did this happen to you, Ky?" she asks, picking up her notepad.

"It's just a hypothetical."

"And you think that, hypothetically, one guy died and one came home, and there's a reason for that?"

"No." My shoulders slump. "Yes. I mean maybe. Like maybe I was supposed to cross paths with somebody that needed me. Like maybe I needed to save her. Madison and I —we're very similar people. We both have shitty pasts, and we're both trying to find a way to change that. Because in the end, I think we're both struggling with the realization that the past doesn't create us." I take a moment, gathering my thoughts. "I don't think it's our pasts that define us, and it's not even our life's final destination. It's everything we do in between, the actual *living*, that creates *who* we are."

* * *

MADISON ENDED UP in my bed last night. We didn't do anything, not physically, but that doesn't mean that we didn't connect. We faced each other, holding tight to what seemed like the only thing that made sense in our world—*us*.

We spoke for a long time, and afterward, we both knew where we stood. For me, I'd give her everything—and in return, she promised to give me as much as she could. And that was enough. For now, and for as long as she needed it to be.

DeLuca called once she'd fallen asleep in my arms. "Meet me at Club Zero in an hour. You can bring that girl of yours." I almost hung up on him and called Jackson. I wanted to tell him to call the whole thing off, that I wanted out. It just didn't seem important at that moment, not after learning about Madison's life.

The case, the need to ruin someone, the revenge—it

seemed so trivial, so insignificant.

Instead, I told DeLuca it wasn't a good night, that my girl-friend wasn't feeling well. "Madison?" he asked after a beat. "Is she sick?" The concern in his voice seemed genuine, and I'd wondered for a moment who the fuck Nate DeLuca was. Who he *really* was. As a person. And why he'd chosen the life of organized crime over anything else.

"No. Not physically," I told him.

He seemed to understand and asked if we could meet the next night. To say that I was surprised was an understate-ment. For the first time since I'd met him, I wondered if he were crazy. Legit, certifiable, bipolar-type crazy.

"Sure," I said, not wanting to push my luck.

I spent the rest of the night deep in my own thoughts. Thoughts of Madison, of me, of us together. And then I did something I never let myself do—I thought about Christine and how much I miss her. How it'd be so easy to pick up the phone and call her. How it would feel to hear her voice. And then I thought about the guilt and the shame that came with all of it, and I just couldn't.

I couldn't take it back.

I couldn't make it right.

And I sure as hell couldn't face her.

No matter how much I want to.

* * *

"So where are we going?" Madison asks, her eyes scanning the numerous dresses she has laid out on my bed.

"Just a club a few blocks from here. We'll catch a cab. It's cold out."

Her gaze moves to mine. "I've never been to a club before."

"Never?"

She shrugs, looking back down at her clothes. "Who are we meeting?"

"Just a friend." I finish slipping on my shoes and kiss her temple. "Just pick one, babe, you look hot in anything."

She smiles. "You choose."

I pick the closest one and hand it to her. "Don't take too long or we're going to be late."

SHE COMES OUT of the bedroom an hour later, and I almost kick myself for not checking her clothes properly. Bright red. Strapless. Hugs every single curve. Barely covers her ass. "Maybe you should change."

"Ky!" she almost yells. "It took me forever to get ready and you chose this—"

"I'm kidding!" *I'm not.* "Let's go before I strip that dress off of you with my teeth."

She raises an eyebrow in challenge.

"Don't tempt me, Maddy."

MADISON GIGGLES THE entire cab ride to the club while watching me squirm in my seat. The way she's dressed and the way she looks at me, added to the way her fucking hand slowly creeps up my thigh... she loves the power. *Thrives* on it.

Me? I'm just doing everything I can to not take her right here and now. "If I get into a fight with an asshole that looks at you the wrong way or looks at you *period*... call Jackson. He'll bail me out."

She laughs, but I'm dead serious. I even make her save Jackson's number in her phone.

Ky: *I'm at Zero.*
DeLuca: *Got caught up, I'll be there in ten.*

I get carded at the door, and the bouncer takes one look at Madison and lets her through.

We walk through a narrow hallway to get to the club doors. "The walls are vibrating," she says, her hand pressed against the wall. The music intensifies tenfold when we step into the club. She stops in her tracks and winces, covering her ears and plastering her face to my chest.

I hold her head in my hands and tilt it back, my eyes scanning her face. "What's wrong?"

"It's too loud!" Her hands press firmer against her ears. "It hurts!"

My eyes narrow in confusion as I take in her state. She looks like she's in genuine pain. I want to leave, but I already told DeLuca I was here. "Do you think you can handle it for fifteen minutes?"

"I think so," she shouts.

"Let's get a drink, okay? It might help." I use my chest to block one of her ears and my hand to cover her other one. At the bar, I order two shots of whiskey and hand one to her. We stay in the same position while we down them. "You okay, babe?"

Her face scrunches in discomfort. I press both my hands to her ears, and she covers them with hers before nodding.

"You're so damn cute," I tell her. She responds by getting on her toes and kissing me quickly. After a moment, her hands loosen and she pulls away. "Another one," I mouth. She smiles, knowing exactly what I want. She kisses again, her hands now on my chest. Mine remain on her ears, hopefully blocking out enough of the music. She slowly relaxes into me, letting me drown in the taste of her. There's a moment of silence while the song changes, but she doesn't notice because her lips stay on mine, curling into a smile as we try to maintain the flow of our kiss—the same flow we're now so accustomed to. Her arms wrap around my waist, bringing me closer to her until a thump on my back has me stumbling forward. We pull apart, just as I shove at the body standing beside me.

Madison squeals, her hands covering her ears again. "What the hell's your problem?" I shout at the person next to me, but my attention's on Madison. I pull her into my chest again, covering her ears with a second barrier.

"I was trying to get your attention," a deep male voice shouts back. I look up to see DeLuca, jaw clenched, eyes narrowed. "Looks like you were both too preoccupied," he says, jerking his head toward her. "What's her problem?"

My shirt hides most of Madison's face, but I can see her eyes squeezed shut. "Can we make this quick?" I ask DeLuca. "It's too loud in here for her. It's hurting her ears."

"Huh," he says, still fixated on her.

"Anytime you want to quit staring at my girlfriend would be *perfect*."

"Sure." He moves his attention to the phone in his hand as he taps away, while I wait impatiently. A few seconds pass before he motions for us to follow him. Madison stays plastered to my side as he leads us to the back of the club and into a soundproof office. I release Madison, and she slowly removes her hands from her ears. We sit down on the couch in the corner of the office while DeLuca watches her intently. "Better?" he asks her.

She nods.

"Do you need a drink or anything?"

She smiles awkwardly. "I'm fine. Thank you."

"You sure?"

I interrupt their little back and forth. "Why did you want to meet?"

He rubs the back of his head and looks at Madison again with an intensity I can't seem to decipher. When his gaze flicks back to me, he blows out a heavy breath and shakes his head. "It's not important, man. I'll text you. Just get her out of here." He taps his phone a few times. "A cab's waiting out back. It saves you from going through the club again."

"Thanks," I say, but all I can think about is the attention he's paying to Madison. A tiny part of me is grateful—the rest of me is pissed.

SHE MENTIONS HER ears are still ringing while we're in a cab heading home. As soon as we get into my apartment, she goes straight to the bedroom. She strips out of her clothes, leaving her in nothing but her bra and panties and climbs into bed, throwing the covers over her head. I pull out my phone and start looking up how to treat ringing ears when a text comes through from DeLuca.

DeLuca: *Call me when you can.*

"Babe, I've got to make a call. Will you be okay?"

Her hand pokes out from under the sheets, and she waves me off.

DELUCA ANSWERS ON the first ring. "Hey."

"What's up?"

"So, I wanted to talk to you about who you'll be fighting."

"Okay?"

"His name's James Hayden. You should be able to find some info on him online. He used to train over at JL Ju-Jitsu."

"Okay, thanks." I'm about to hang up, but then I think *fuck it*. I'd rather deal with this shit now than let it eat away at me. "I wanted to talk to you about something else."

"Yeah?" he asks.

I give it to him straight. "I'm not happy with the way you are around Maddy."

"Maddy?"

"Yeah. Madison. My *girlfriend*. You can't seem to take your eyes off her, and to be honest, it pisses me off and makes her uncomfortable."

Dead silence greets me on the other end.

I fear I may have fucked up, gotten too personal, but after a long-ass moment, I hear him sigh. "You're right," he says. And I find myself both relieved and surprised. He adds, "I apologize."

"Okay, good talk," I mumble.

"It's just that she reminds me of someone I used to know. The resemblance is fucking uncanny."

"You think you used to know her?"

"No. Not Madison. I don't know her at all."

His words confuse me, but before I can say anything, he says, "I'll be out of town until your fight, got business to take care of, so you probably won't hear from me until then."

"Okay."

"All right, Parker. I'll see ya."

I hang up and stare down at my phone. Even though something feels off about the way he'd spoken to me, there's absolutely no trace of threats in his words, no form of authority.

I CALL JACKSON, who's already expecting my call, and I give him the details of the meetup. I leave out the parts about Maddy, just like I leave out the parts of me that are really starting to wonder about DeLuca, about the case, and whether it's worth it.

But then Jackson thanks me, tells me how much he appreciates everything I'm doing. And just like that, I decide that Jackson and what he wants—what *we* want—is more important than what *I'm* feeling.

So I decide to put him first.

Because he earned it.

And after everything he and his family have done for me, he sure as shit deserves it.

22
KY

FOR THE LAST four days, I've woken up with Madison sleeping peacefully next to me, and every morning I question the exact same thing: what the hell could be better than this? And the answer is and probably always will be: *nothing*.

Absolutely nothing.

HER EYES ARE closed, but the corners of her lips curl. "Are you watching me again?"

"No. How creepy would that be?"

Her eyes snap open and she rolls on her back, eying me sideways. "Liar."

I shrug in response, then lean up on my elbow so I can look her in the eyes when she reaches up, her fingers finding my dog tags hanging just above her breasts. I do my best to glance at them inconspicuously, but my hand has a mind of its own. I trace a slow line from her chin, down her neck to her chest, rising and falling, matching her heavy breaths. I move my finger lower and lower, waiting for her to tell me to stop, but she doesn't have to, because her phone sounds, causing us to pull apart.

I leave her to read her text while I shower, and when I

return, she's still looking down at her phone, her mind distant. "Everything okay?" I ask.

She sits up and drops the phone to the side. "Yup," she says, nodding. And even though I suspect she's lying, I don't push her. I don't feel the need to.

Her phone sounds again but she ignores it, opting instead to kiss me goodbye. "You want to pick me up from Debbie's shop when you're done?" she asks.

"Sure. But hold out on getting your frames today, okay? I want to pick some with you."

Her smile's huge. "Okay!"

I stare at her a moment longer before I force myself to look away and then walk away, because each day spent together just makes it harder to be without her.

* * *

Sara: *I miss you.*
Sara: *Message me when you get this. I'm worried.*

* * *

I TRY TO be quiet as I walk into Debbie's Flowers, but Madison hears me anyway. She smiles and continues to water some flowers on the back wall.

Picking up a single orange rose on the way over to her, I press my chest against her back and set my hand on her stomach, then lift the rose to her nose. "Orange?" She laughs. "You know that means lust and desire?"

"Good. That's what I was going for."

I kiss her neck, smiling against it when she tilts her head to give me better access.

Debbie clears her throat from behind us.

"Sorry," I say, turning to her. "She's kind of irresistible."

There's amusement in Debbie's eyes when she asks, "What are your plans for the rest of the day, Kyler?"

I fake a sigh. "Not a lot, Debbie. Just hanging out with a girl I'm in lust with."

Madison scoffs.

I continue, "Actually, I do have plans. But it's a surprise."

Madison smiles up at me. "Surprise? I like surprises."

"Yeah? I'm hoping you like what I have to offer a lot more than your stupid mailbox."

WE WALK BACK to our building and check my mail. I pray Jackson's made good on his word and smile when my fingers skim the metal of a key. "What's that?" Madison asks.

"Jax being fucking awesome is what it is," I answer, taking her hand. I lead her down the stairs to the basement parking garage and look at the car logo on the key—*Ford*—and I start to press the keyless entry remote, listening for the sound.

"Oh my God," she yelps, running toward the car. Only it's not just any car; it's a blue Mustang GT convertible—and the roof's already down.

"Get in!" I shout.

She doesn't hesitate.

I take my time and pull out my phone to send Jackson a text.

> *Ky:* Holy shit! This is your car?
> *Jackson:* I wish. It came from the impound lot at the station so be careful!
> *Ky:* How the fuck did you manage that?
> *Jackson:* I'm screwing the girl in charge.
> *Ky:* Shut up! You didn't tell me you were dating.

*Jackson: I didn't say we were dating. I said I was
screwing her. There's a difference, big brother.*
Ky: That's BADASS, Jax.
Jackson: I'm serious about not messing it up.
Ky: You got it. You sly motherfucker you.
Jackson: Enjoy, asshole.

"Where are we going?" she asks, bouncing in her seat as I get in the car.

"Quiet, you!"

She glares at me.

I turn the key in the ignition, then lean back against the headrest, relishing in the purr of the engine. "That's the sound of over six hundred fifty horsepower, babe."

Her face forms to a look of disgust. "Are you..." She reaches over to cover my crotch.

Laughing, I smack her hand away.

"You're hard, aren't you?" she jokes. "You should have sex with it."

"I may as well have sex with something," I retort.

Her jaw drops, her eyes huge. "You—I-I can't believe you just said that!"

I laugh harder and kiss her quickly. She pulls away, feigning anger. "Another one," I say.

She rolls her eyes but caves and kisses me again. Then she covers my face with her hand and pushes me away. "It's not like you've ever made a move," she mumbles.

I don't respond, because she's right, and I won't push her to do anything until she's ready to give me all of her. Anything less and it won't do us justice.

"Okay, so please don't get too excited," I warn. "It's really not that great. In fact, you'll probably think it's dumb. But just pretend that you like it. For me, okay?"

"I'm with you, right? That's enough." She places her hand

on my leg and squeezes once. "That will always be enough, Ky."

THERE ARE NO signs on the warehouse, which makes the surprise even better. We wait for a few people to exit the building before stepping inside.

She gasps, then grips my arm tight, before releasing an all-consuming laugh. "This is amazing!" She practically runs past the registers and down the first aisle. "How did you find this place?" she asks, picking up a frame.

All I see when I look around are aisles upon aisles of nothing but picture frames. "It's like an overstock warehouse," I tell her. "So this will be here for a few weeks. I know right before Christmas they fill it with decorations."

"This place should exist for eternity!" she squeals.

She picks up a few frames and inspects the pictures inside, before setting them back on the shelf.

"You better make quick choices, Maddy. We don't have all day."

Her eyes widen as if new life's just been pumped into her.

I laugh. "I'll get a basket."

"You better get a cart!"

THREE GODDAMN HOURS.

That's how long we spent looking at nothing but frames. Most dudes would've walked out after a half hour and her constant indecisiveness. Call me a chump, but I was just as into it as she was.

Now came the best part.

The *real* surprise.

We drive a few miles east, and as soon as she realizes where we are, she starts to fidget in her seat. We park the car and start walking toward the center of Logan Circle, a park in Center City. She keeps her head down and stays quiet, right up until we're a few yards away from the fountain in the middle of the park. Then she stops in her tracks and turns to me. "Okay," she breathes, pushing back her shoulders and shaking out her hands. "I have to tell you something."

I wait.

And wait. And then finally break the silence. "What's going on?"

"This place—I'm just a little unsure of what I'm feeling right now."

I take her hands and hold them. "Why?"

"It's just that—you know how I told you about that stuff?"

I watch a million different emotions flash in her eyes. "Yeah..."

"I've spent a lot of nights here... sleeping in this park."

Shit. "I'm sorry. We can go. I just thought—"

"No." She tries to laugh, but her need to cry is greater. "I'm not telling you because I want your pity or because I want to leave. I'm telling you because until right now—this place—it held a completely different meaning for me. And until you came along, Ky, so did everything else."

She places her hand on the back of my neck, bringing me down to her waiting lips. The warmth of her tears spreads on my cheek as I eagerly return her kiss. The want to say what we can't voice is beyond need, beyond desperation. She pulls back, her eyes glazed but her smile in place as her arm settles around my waist, and she leads us to the fountain.

I stay quiet. Because really? What the hell am I supposed to say?

WE REMAIN CONNECTED as we watch the large streams of water shoot out of the three large cement sculptures. A few kids play in the bottom of the fountain, their laughter bringing out my own. "You know..." she says quietly, "...if you asked me a few months ago to describe this place, it wouldn't be this."

"How would you describe it now?"

Slowly, she turns to me, and even though she smiles to cover it up, I can still see the sadness, the struggle to admit what she says next. "I don't want to feel trapped anymore, Ky. And I know that doesn't make sense to you." She closes her eyes and tilts her head back, letting the heat of the sun warm her face. "It's kind of amazing when you think about it, though. There's all of this to experience," she opens her eyes and smiles wider, then circles her finger in the air, "and all you have to do is *exist*."

I keep my eyes on her. "Exist? It's that simple, huh?"

Her smile turns to a smirk. Then she grabs my arm, pulling me with her until her feet, shoes and all, are in the water. "And make waves!"

I laugh, stepping in with her. She releases my arm so she can spin around in the water, her legs kicking out, splashing at anything and everything.

"You're crazy!" I shout.

She stops, pouts, and steps to me. "I'm crazy?" she asks.

I hold the side of her face, tilting her head up. "You're crazy beautiful." I seal her pout with a kiss while my ears fill with the sound of water running, of kids laughing, of the world going on around us. And I realize it now—there is one thing better than waking up to Madison in my bed.

It's *existing* with Madison.

And, yes, it really is *that* simple.

A THROAT CLEARING has us pulling apart. Madison hides her face in my chest while I look over at the sound. I think we're about to get scolded for our public display of maybe a little too much affection, but a middle-aged woman just smiles at us, curling her finger at me.

I take Madison's hand and walk over to her. "I hope you

don't think I was intruding," the woman says, lifting her phone for me to view. "It was just too good a memory not to capture." I take the phone from her hand and look at the picture she'd taken. And there we are, kissing in front of the fountain, arms around each other. And at that moment, we ignored everything else. There was no outside world. We were it. And it was just like the couple from the first frame we bought.

You know—the ones who met in the foyer of their building...

The ones who ended up living opposite each other...

The ones who used pizza as a way to get closer...

I laugh and show Madison.

She covers her mouth with her hand and flicks her gaze between the phone and me.

"Look at that," I say, my eyes on hers. "We're loving freely."

MADISON

I USED TO close my eyes and try to imagine what it would be like... to feel a breeze through my hair... hear the sounds of existence... to feel unrestricted.

If I knew it would feel like this—this *good*—I never would've opened my eyes.

23
KY

THE WOMAN SENT the picture to my phone, and Madison and I spent the rest of the afternoon taking selfies. She snorted when I said the word "selfies," like the word didn't really exist. I was about to laugh at her and ask if she'd been living under a rock for the last few years, but then I realized —maybe she actually had been...living under a rock, I mean. It would explain why she seemed to have no clue what the hell Facebook was.

Of course, I'm curious about what had changed—and how she's managing to rent an apartment when she's unemployed. But my feelings for her completely outweigh my curiosity.

MADISON'S BEEN QUIET on the drive home, so I figure she's just thinking about the day—hopefully thinking about me, just like I'm thinking about her. It's almost dusk when we stop by a photo-printing kiosk to print off all the pictures we'd taken from my phone. "I can't believe this is what I look like!" she says at one point.

I ask her how she doesn't know what she looks like. She just shrugs and sits down next to me, her head on my shoulder while she waits for me to go through them all.

"You okay?" I ask.

"Yeah," she whispers. "I'm just tired."

I kiss her forehead, tasting the sweat that's formed. She blinks a few times, trying to focus her gaze. "You sure you're okay?"

She smiles and nods. "Let's just print them and take them home. We can look at them there."

She sits in silence for a good five minutes while I curse at the photo machine that keeps fucking up. "Ky," she whispers.

I stab my finger on the touch screen, annoyed at its lack of cooperation.

"Ky," she says again.

"Yeah?" I answer, distracted.

"I don't feel well."

I quickly turn to her. All color has drained from her face, and she's covered in sweat. Her breaths are short and sharp, her head drooping like she doesn't have the energy to hold it up. I squat down in front of her while she struggles to keep her eyes open. "Ky," she whimpers, and my heart stops. "I need..."

"What, baby? What do you need?"

She swallows, but it looks like a struggle. "I'm dizzy."

"Okay." I try to stay calm—for her. On the inside, I'm breaking. "Let's just get you home, okay?"

She does her best to nod.

I grasp her hand and try to help her stand, but she's dead weight in my arms and falls back in her chair. "You have to tell me what to do, baby. What's wrong? What can I do?"

"I need..."

I hold her head in my hands and search her face. "Need what, Maddy? Talk to me!"

She weeps and pushes my hands away, then tries to stand again. She only gets halfway before she grasps her seat and uses it to soften her fall to the floor, letting out another sob.

I link my fingers behind my head and look back down at her. She's almost lying on the floor now. "I don't know what to do, Maddy." I pull out my phone and start to dial 911. "I'm calling an ambulance."

Her hand shoots up. "No, Ky! Please." She cries harder.

"Why!"

She shakes her head. "Please."

The store clerk rushes up and stands beside me. "Is she okay?"

"I don't know!" I almost shout. My panic spikes as I see Madison's eyes drifting shut. The clerk squats in front of her and holds two fingers to her wrist, her other hand going to her forehead.

"What are you doing?" I ask, even though I know the answer; she's doing what I *should* been doing, but I'm too terrified to think straight.

"My name's Paula," the clerk says. "I'm pre-med over at Jefferson. I can show you my ID."

I wave her off. "It's fine."

"What's her name?"

I squat down next to Paula and take Madison's other hand. I choke on my words but regain enough composure to answer her. "Madison. Her name's Madison."

"Did she say if she has trouble breathing?" Paula asks.

"No. She said she was dizzy. She's sweating though, and she keeps blinking."

"Madison?" Paula croons, rubbing her hand along Madison's forehead. "Can you hear me okay?"

Madison lifts her head, then lets it drop again.

"Do you know what's happening to her?"

Paula ignores me, instead ordering me to get a can of soda and an energy bar from the vending machine. I do what she asks, tearing the packet open on my way back.

"Madison?" Paula says again. "Are you diabetic?"

Madison whimpers a "yes" before mumbling something that makes absolutely no sense to me.

Luckily, Paula understands. "Insulin?" she asks, helping Madison sit up. Paula gives her the energy bar.

Madison chews it slowly while Paula turns to me. "When was she supposed to take her insulin?"

My stomach drops to the floor, along with the rest of me, as I kneel in front of Madison. "Maddy... what are you talking about? What insulin?"

Madison throws her head back, lifting the energy bar and biting into it.

"I didn't know," I mumble.

Paula offers Madison the now-open soda. "Has she eaten today?" Paula asks me.

"I think so. I mean, we skipped lunch—"

"She can't skip meals if she's diabetic. This is what happens."

"I didn't know," I repeat, looking back at Madison. "She didn't tell me."

Madison's gaze lifts to mine, her eyes pleading. Her bottom lip quivers as she forces herself to swallow and take a sip of her drink.

"Where's your insulin?" Paula asks her. "Is it in your bag?"

I turn my back on both of them.

"Apartment," Madison whispers. Then louder, "Ky?"

"Yeah?" I say, still unable to look at her.

"I'm okay," she squeaks. "This isn't your fault."

My phone sounds, giving me reason to pretend like I didn't hear her.

Jackson: *When are you bringing the car back?*
Ky: *I can't. Madison. There's something wrong with her. I don't know what to do.*
Jackson: *Where are you?*

Ky: *Picture Perfect on Eighth.*

When I return my attention to Madison, Paula's saying, "You've been out in the sun all day, dehydrated, and you haven't eaten or had your insulin. This could have been really bad, Madison."

"I know," she answers, her hands trembling as she brings the soda to her mouth.

Paula stands in front of me. "She needs to go home. She needs to eat. And you need to monitor her sugar level, make sure it doesn't spike too high or too low. And you should probably get her a diabetes bracelet, too. Just so people are aware if or when this happens to her again."

I try to take in all her words, try to remember in detail everything she just said. "Thank you," I rush out. "If you weren't here... I don't know what the hell I would have done."

"Hey," Paula croons, rubbing my arm. "If you don't know what the signs are, you can't be expected to know how to react."

"You're a lifesaver."

She shoves her hands in her back pockets and rocks on her heels. And then she smiles. "You're welcome...?"

"Ky."

Her smile gets wider. "It was nice meeting you, Ky. I mean... under the circumstances and all."

Madison clears her throat, her brow bunched as she looks up at me.

I sigh and sit down next to her. "You scared me," I tell her, linking our hands.

She doesn't respond.

Jackson shows up in a squad car, sirens blaring.

"Why are the cops here?" Madison asks, panic clear in her voice.

"It's just Jax."

"He's a cop?"

"Detective," I tell her, watching Jax walk in, his shoulders squared, eyes narrowed.

He seems to settle down when he sees us. "How are you doing, Madison?" he asks, stopping and squatting in front of us.

"I'll be okay," she says, resting her head on my shoulder.

He nods once and then turns to me. "What happened?"

"She's diabetic," I manage to get out.

He looks back at Madison. "You need me to take you to the hospital? You can ride in the squad car."

She straightens up quickly and shakes her head. "No!" Then she takes a few calming breaths and adds, "Honestly, Jackson, thank you, but I'm fine. I just need to go home."

He rears back a little, startled by her response. When his eyes find mine, I shake my head. I don't want him questioning her or pushing her too much. I'll be doing enough of that later.

I reach into my pocket and hand Jackson the car keys. "Are you able to give us a ride?"

"Yeah. Of course."

He makes his way back to the squad car and speaks to the driver through the window. The car disappears a moment later, and I look at Madison sipping slowly on her soda. "We need to talk about this, Maddy. I'm serious."

* * *

I LEAN AGAINST her bathroom counter with my arms crossed while she shows me her medicine bag. "So how much do you use? I mean... are there different doses depending on... I don't even know what the fuck to ask right now."

"Ky, it's fine. I have it under control."

I scoff and roll my eyes. "Clearly."

"Don't be mad. We had a good day today."

"Yeah, we did. And then you could have died."

"Don't be dramatic."

I throw my hands in the air and push off the counter. "What if Paula wasn't there?"

"Oh *Paula*," she says, her nose scrunching in disgust.

"What?"

"Yeah. She loved you."

"Shut up!"

Her eyes widen in shock. "What!"

"I'm fucking serious right now, Maddy. Don't joke around."

Her shoulders sag, and she exhales loudly, her breath shaky while she continues to pack away her stuff. Then she turns to me but doesn't speak.

And for a moment, neither do I.

Our eyes lock, waiting for the other to crack first.

I won't cave. Not this time.

"I'm sorry," she finally says.

"You scared me."

"I know."

Taking a step toward her, I try for an even tone when I say, "You know I'm not going to push you to talk about certain things, but stuff like this—I need to know about it. I need to know what to do if this happens again or what I need to do to prevent it from happening in the first place."

"I—"

"Don't say you had it under control, Madison, because that's a fucking lie."

"I was just going to say that I forgot. I was having such a good time that I honestly forgot about it. And then we got in the car, and I started—"

"You should have told me right away."

"I didn't want you to worry!"

"Like I am right now?"

She groans, frustrated. "Can you at least yell at me after I eat?"

* * *

I RAISE MY eyebrows at her, jerking my head at her plate. "Keep going," I snap.

She rolls her eyes and makes a show of chewing and swallowing her food. "Ky, I'm not a kid."

I cross my arms. "When the plate's empty, we're going to sit down and you're going to walk me through everything. Step by step."

She drops her fork and matches my stance, then mumbles under her breath.

I lean forward on my elbows, waiting until I'm calm before I speak. "Don't you think you're being unfair?"

She scoffs. "Me! Have you met *you* right now? How can you say *I'm* being unfair?"

"Because you are, Madison. You're being unfair to *us*. You were right. We had a great day, and it could have ended great if you'd just told me what was going on instead of hiding it from me." I pause, waiting for her to speak up, but she doesn't. "You're not being fair to us and whatever it is we are at the moment, because you and I—we're just beginning, and with what you did today, you're not giving us a chance. And I *want* that chance. Don't you, babe? Don't you think we deserve that? To be happy? Because you *do*, Maddy—you make me happy. And seeing you the way you were today—" I push down the lump in my throat, my eyes on her as she stares down at the table. "I don't want to see you like that again. And I don't want to be helpless with you. I want to take care of you, no matter what it is... but you have to be honest with me, at least with that. *Please*."

She looks up—a perfect pout formed on her perfect lips, but she isn't faking it this time. She nods and picks up her fork.

We spend the rest of her meal in silence.

When she's done, she stands up and offers me her hand. Then she leads me back to her bathroom. She tells me all about her diabetes—what type it is and the things she does to keep it under control. She says that she hasn't had any issues since she's moved in and that today was the first time anything like that has happened.

She then guides me through her insulin doses and even shows me the tiny dots that cover parts of her stomach and both her thighs from the needles. Marks that, even though I've spent a lot of time up close and personal with her body, I've never noticed before. She also mentions that she hopes I don't find those things unattractive. I tell her she's stupid and that if she thinks that then she doesn't know me at all. And then I ask her something that's been bugging me since we left the photo kiosk. "Why didn't you want to go to the hospital, Maddy?"

She shrugs and averts her gaze. "I can't afford it."

"Bullshit. You know I would've covered you."

"I don't want your money."

I pull on her arm until she's standing in front of me. Then I lift her chin with my finger, giving her no choice but to look at me. "And I don't want your lies."

Her throat bobs once, her shoulders sagging when she gives up to the inevitable. "Because I don't exist, Ky. Not officially. My dad forgot about me when I was twelve, and I packed whatever I could and ended up on the streets at fifteen. It's not like I have a driver's license or anything."

"But now? I mean—"

"Ky!" She's almost begging now. "I'm tired," she cries. "And I just want to go to sleep. And I want to forget the last part of the day. Please? Can we just talk about this tomorrow?"

"Fine. But we're—"

"I know!" she shouts. "I get it. You're mad. You're disappointed. Just please... not now." Her voice breaks into a sob, giving me everything I need to quit being a dick.

"You're right, babe. I'm sorry."

"Will you kiss me now?" she asks, her head tilting all the way back. She scrunches her nose and exaggerates the puckering of her lips. I try not to smile. I fail. And the second our lips make contact, she circles her arms around me, keeping me in place. We kiss until we fall on her bed, but I stop it before it can go any further. "You need to rest."

She rolls her eyes but agrees.

She invites me to stay in her apartment so she has access to everything she needs just in case. Of course, I agree. But I don't sleep. I spend the first couple of hours watching her like a hawk and, when I'm confident enough that she's fine, I go to my apartment and get my laptop. I return to her bed and quietly press on the keys, researching everything I can about diabetes, specifically type two, and the medication and treatment needed. Turns out there are four different types of insulin. They all take different times to reach the blood stream and have different durations of effect. I don't recall her telling me what types she uses, so I go to her bathroom to check the label on the bottle.

There's a label on there, but it isn't her name on the prescription.

Mr. Mark Wade.

Who the fuck is Mark Wade?

24
KY

I CALL JACKSON and tell him I want to take a few days off training to keep an eye on Madison. He says he understands, but I can hear in his voice that he isn't happy about it. Then he asks me a question that I knew was coming. "Why didn't she want an ambulance?"

"It wasn't that bad," I lie, moving around Madison's kitchen to make her breakfast.

"Bullshit, Ky. I know you. I saw your face when I got there. You were rocked."

I shrug, even though he can't see me. "Maybe she doesn't have insurance and can't afford it. Who knows?"

"You didn't question it?"

"No. Why would I?"

He stays silent.

I sigh. "Just leave it alone, Jax. I don't need this shit from you on top of everything else."

"Fine. Have you heard from DeLuca?"

"Not since the club."

"And you think you're ready?"

"I will be."

The bedroom door opens and Madison steps out, her eyes roaming her apartment.

"Babe," I call out. She smiles when she sees me and makes her way over.

"I like you in my kitchen," she says, rising to her toes and kissing me quickly.

"Give me a call if you hear anything," Jackson says, hanging up before I have a chance to respond.

I drop my phone on the counter and lift Madison onto the counter next to it. Palms flat on either side of her, I ask, "How are you feeling?"

She rests her forearms on my shoulders. "Honestly?"

"Yes."

"I'm still a little weak, but I'll have my insulin and something to eat and we can go from there." Even though I know she said it for my benefit, it's the answer I need.

"So..." I start apprehensively. "Who's Mark Wade?"

At first, she's confused, then her eyes go wide with understanding. She sighs and pushes my arm away and hops off the counter to walk around me. "You went through my stuff?" she mumbles.

"A: you willingly showed me your stuff and B: should we really be talking about who goes through whose stuff?"

She starts to set the table and speaks to me with her back turned. "Do you know how hard it is to find a doctor when you're homeless? Or how expensive medication is when you can't even afford a meal?"

"So it's not legit?"

"The medication is legit. How it's obtained isn't. I don't know who Mark Wade is—but whoever he is, he helps me get cheap insulin."

"You need to—"

She turns swiftly, her eyes already narrowed. "No, Ky. I don't need to do anything! You promised! You said you wouldn't push me until I was ready and I'm not!" Her eyes lose focus, and she gasps for breath. I get to her quickly, pulling out a chair that she practically collapses into.

I squat in front of her. "I'm sorry."

"Can you just—I know this is hard—I get that. And I'm sorry that you have to put up with me."

"Stop it."

"No, Ky. If this ever gets to be too much for you—my past, my secrets, and now your need to be overly protective—you know where the door is. You don't owe me anything."

"Don't say that, Maddy; I wouldn't be here if I didn't want to be... if I didn't care about you. I'm just worried—"

"I just feel like you're interrogating me all the time now, and I don't like it. I just want to go back to—"

"Existing?" I cut in.

"Yes."

I nod. "Okay."

* * *

WHEN I TOLD Madison I was taking a few days off, she said I was overreacting, but she was happy she'd have me all to herself for a while. We take it easy, only leaving the apartment for a couple of hours at a time. We cook meals together instead of eating out every night, which I'm sure didn't help with her diet.

It was a give and take. A push and pull. I wanted to take care of her—she wanted the freedom to take care of herself. But the truth? I loved being the one to look after her and I think she knew that, which is why she seemed to take a lot more than she gave.

"YOU TAKE GOOD care of me, Kyler," she says, stroking my hair as I rest my head on her stomach.

She's watching TV. I'm discreetly on my phone, looking

up how to obtain an ID for someone that has no prior proof of identity. It's important she gets the right treatment—regardless of what she says. "I like taking care of you. It makes me feel important," I mumble.

"Is Christine like that? The nursing type?"

"Yeah." I wasn't getting anywhere with my online search. I know I have the best resource at my fingertips, but Jackson's my last resort. It's bad enough I'm missing training—he doesn't need to know how truly distracted I've become.

"Do you miss her?" she asks.

"Yeah," I answer, my mind elsewhere.

AFTER A FEW minutes of silence and me reading the same websites over and over—I finally cave.

Ky: *Hey. I need a favor.*
Jackson: *Anything.*

* * *

Madison: *I need a favor.*
Jackson: *Who is this?*
Madison: *Madison.*
Jackson: *What do you need?*

25

KY

Dr. Aroma stares at me.

I stare back.

Her eyes narrow a little.

I squirm under her gaze.

"What?" she asks.

I look around the room, wondering if she's speaking to me, because I haven't said a word. There's no one else here. "I didn't say anything."

"Oh."

"Are you okay, Doc?"

"I'm fine." She pours a glass of water, then downs the entire thing in one swig, her eyes staying on mine.

I wait until she's set the glass back down and ask, "Do you think relationships can work if there are secrets involved?"

"Ah ha!" she almost shouts, pointing her finger at me.

I rear back in surprise and stupidly look around the room again.

She clears her throat. "Carry on."

"Okay..." I eye her sideways before continuing. "I guess I'm just wondering how important it is to share absolutely everything. And if the feeling of suspicion will always linger because you know the person is holding back."

Dr. Aroma sits forward a little, her gaze penetrating mine even more. "I don't know, Ky," she says, her eyes thinning to slits. "Depends on what the secret is and if it involves the skanky whore that runs the impound lot at the police station."

I stifle my laugh and trap my lips between my teeth, watching her eyes widen with her sudden admission. "Time's up," she says.

"I just sat down."

"You're excused."

"No." I shake my head and cross my arms, loving the switch in power. "I think I'm going to sit here and talk. You can stay silent if you want. Or you can talk."

She matches my stance. "Fine."

"So today I think I'm going take a page from your book and talk about all of my best friend's crushes when he was in high school. You may know him as Detective Davis..."

* * *

I WAKE UP the next morning in an empty bed.

Quickly, I get up and search my apartment for Madison, but she isn't there. Neither is her bag. I check my phone. There are no missed calls. No messages. My heart stops. I dial her number. She picks up on the fourth ring. "Hey, babe!"

"Jesus Christ, Maddy, where the hell are you?"

"Just went to see Debbie."

"You should have sent a text—"

She laughs. "I left you a note."

"Who the hell leaves notes these days!"

She laughs harder. "I'll be back soon. You better have

calmed down by then because I'm not putting up with grumpy Ky all day."

Just as I'm about to respond, there's a knock on the door. Figuring it's Madison, I open the door in my boxers—half-mast.

"Dude!" Jackson yells, shielding his eyes from my dick. "Put that thing away."

"I'll call you back," I tell Madison, then hang up. I leave the door open for Jackson and go to the bedroom to put on some clothes. "What are you doing here?" I yell out.

I hear the front door close and then the TV switch on. "I have no idea," he shouts back.

Once my pants are on and I've shrugged on a shirt, I join him on the couch. "What the hell do you mean you have no idea?"

"Your girl messaged me—asked me to meet her here." He looks around the apartment. "Where is she, anyway?"

"Out."

He mutes the TV. "She's not here?"

"Nope."

He taps my chest with the back of his hand, and when I turn to him, he says, "So I have that info you asked for, but I don't know how you're going to react to it."

"Hit me."

"She doesn't exist—Madison Haynes—at least not anyone that matches her description."

I rub my jaw and puff out a breath. "I kind of knew that already."

"You knew?"

"Well yeah, that's why I asked you. But I thought you'd be able to find a birth certificate... something."

"Ky, I searched. I can't find shit about anyone with that name, and what the hell do you mean you knew?"

"I can't tell you," I cut in. "It's not my story to tell, Jax."

"Fine. But there's more."

My attention peaks. "More?"

"So I looked into the lease on her apartment..."

"And?"

"It was paid three months in advance... cash. And the name on the lease? *Cash*."

I shrug. "That's not a big deal. I mean, maybe that's all she could afford. It's not like she has a credit history or social security."

He shakes his head. "What are you not telling me, Ky?"

"Like I said, not my story."

"But it could be dangerous—"

The front door opens and Madison steps in, grinning like the damn Cheshire cat when she sees both of us on the couch. "Good. You're both here."

I would respond, if not for the fact that I can't comprehend why the hell she's holding a bouquet of white lilies.

She stands in front of the TV, placing a plastic bag and the lilies on the coffee table. And then... *nothing*. She just stands there smiling at the both of us.

I look over at Jax, but he's focused on her. With a sigh, I stand up and take the steps to get to Madison. I grip her arm and turn my back on Jax so he can't hear me whisper, "What the hell are the white lilies for? And why did you ask Jackson to come here?"

She pulls back a little so she can look up at me. "Well..." she sings, "the white lilies go with this." She reaches over to the bag on the table and pulls out a wooden picture frame, the word 'MOM' etched on the top. "Look," she says, her grin still displayed. She points to the picture of an older woman with two young men standing on either side. "It could be you and Jax."

Jax chuckles.

I glare at him, then give my attention back to Madison. "And what's he here for?"

"He's my backup."

"Your backup?" I ask incredulously.

"Yes, Ky, we're going to visit Christine today—"

"No, we're not!"

She flinches slightly. "And Jackson's here to help me convince you."

I direct my gaze at Jackson. He holds his hands up in surrender, leans back into the couch, stretches his arms on the back of it, and kicks his feet up on the table. Then he shakes his head and waves a hand at us. "Carry on," he states.

I drag Madison by her arm into the bedroom and shut the door. "What the hell are you doing?"

She sits on the edge of the bed, a perfect frown on her face. "It's time, Ky."

"You don't get to decide that, Maddy."

"Maybe not," she says quietly, uncertainty in her eyes for the first time since she walked in. "I'm sorry if I'm overstepping." She hugs her waist. "I just know that I'd give anything to see my mother—or even have one that would want to see me."

My words catch in my throat while she just sits there, staring at me with pity in her eyes. Like I—out of the two of us—am deserving of pity. I sit next to her. "Are you doing this for me or you, Maddy?"

"Neither," she says. "I'm doing it for Christine and Jackson."

Her hand moves slowly down my arm, capturing my hand in hers. "We don't have to go. I just thought..." she trails off.

"You thought what?" I ask, turning back to her.

"Wouldn't it be nice, Ky? To be able to see her, for the three of you to be together again, mend some bridges or whatever. Christmas is coming up. We could spend it with them. You know... as a family."

I can't help but smile. "You're still going to want me in a few months when Christmas rolls around?"

"I'm always going to want you, Kyler Parker."

* * *

I PUSH JACKSON'S feet off the coffee table. "You're driving."

"Like I had a choice."

26

KY

It takes us a half hour to drive to my childhood home.

Jackson starts to slow when we pass my old house and then parks in front of Christine's.

By now, my thoughts are in overdrive; my palms have formed a sheen of sweat and my heart is racing. "It'll be okay," Madison assures me from the back seat.

"There she is," Jackson says, jerking his head out the window.

And there she is—on her knees in the front yard, tending to the garden. It's like time hasn't changed her at all. I sniff the air—which seems stupid at the time, but doing so brings back all the memories I've tried hard to suppress.

"Whenever you're ready, man. We're in no rush," Jax says, and I nod, thankful that he understands my hesitation.

"Here," Madison says, grabbing my attention. I hold her gaze a moment while she offers the lilies to me, hoping that somehow her confidence in the situation will rub off on me. My face presses firmer against her hand when she cups my cheek. Her eyes, glassy with tears, stay fixed on mine. And then she smiles. "All you have to do is exist," she says.

My eyes drift shut. "Exist?"

I feel her lean forward, and the next second, her mouth lands gently on mine. "Just exist," she whispers, pulling back.

I keep my eyes closed. "Another one," I say.

She laughs once and gives me what I want—what I didn't know I *needed*.

* * *

I WALK UP the driveway, glancing back at Jackson and Madison, who are now watching from outside the car. Then I look at Christine—her back to me, her head down, humming something about bass and treble. Through my nerves, my anticipation, and my fear, I somehow manage to smile. I stop a few feet behind her and take one more look at Madison. "Breathe," she mouths. So I do, and after the third breath, I finally gain the courage. "Ma..."

Her hands stop mid-movement, her head slowly lifting. She sets her tools to the side and sits back on her heels. Then her shoulders shake; her hands cover her face, muffling the sound of her sobs.

"Ma," I say again, my voice strained. I stay in my spot, afraid of how she'll react if I move closer—if I touch her. But what I really want to do is hug her. Tell her that I love her and that I miss the absolute shit out of her. And that I'm sorry.

I'm so damn sorry.

She sobs again, slowly coming to a stand.

"Say it again," she whimpers, her back still to me.

"Ma," I say, louder this time.

She turns to me, her cheeks wet from her tears. "Kyler!" She takes two steps forward before falling to her knees—and I'm right there with her, holding her, squeezing her tight.

"I love you, Ma. So much."

She sobs harder.

"And I miss you."

She doesn't stop crying, but they aren't tears of anger or disappointment like I'd thought. They're tears of joy, maybe even a little relief.

I help her to stand but keep her close.

She offers me her cheek. "Give me a kiss!"

I kiss it.

"Another one," she says, offering the other.

I kiss that one, too.

Then she pulls back, clasping her hands in front of her. She scans me from head to toe, then flicks my dog tags. "We have a lot to catch up on."

"I'm sorry, Ma." And as soon as the words leave my mouth, I feel lighter. Who'd have thought that two words— *I'm sorry*—could weigh so heavily on me?

"Shut up, Kyler," she says, her tone clipped. "Let's go inside, son." She flattens her palm on my back and leads me up the path to the front door.

A loud whistle startles us both, and we turn around. Jackson's leaning on his car, his arms crossed. "What about me?" he shouts.

"Jackson!" she squeals. "Get over here!"

He practically runs up the driveway and lifts her off her feet, spinning her in a slow circle. "You're such a goof," she says through a laugh. "Put me down!" She kisses his cheek when he sets her back down.

"How are you, Mom?" Jax asks.

Christine glances at me. "I have my two boys," she says. "Life's damn near perfect!"

I hear Madison's voice. Quiet. Timid. "Ky?"

I look back at the car, but she's no longer there. She's at

the end of the driveway, hesitating to come closer. She presses her hand down her dress and shuffles on her feet, one hand carrying the frame, the other wiping her tears.

Christine squeezes between Jackson and me, taking Madison in for the first time. "Oh wow," Christine says.

Yeah, I get it. Madison—she's kind of breathtaking.

Madison checks her hair and then pushes her shoulders back, trying to appear confident, but she looks so lost. So unsure. So imperfectly perfect.

She checks her hair again, and I chuckle. "You look beautiful, babe," I call, making my way over to her. I hear Christine whisper something to Jax and him agreeing with her.

Taking her hand, I lead her back to Christine. Madison's hand slowly moves between the two of them. "It's a p-pleasure to m-meet you, Mrs. D-Davis."

Christine's gaze flicks from Madison to me. And then a face-splitting grin appears. She ignores Madison's hand and pulls her in for a hug—an extremely long hug. Christine starts to release her but changes her mind at the last second and squeezes her tighter.

Jackson laughs from behind them. "This is why I don't bring girls home, Mom," he teases.

Christine's laugh bubbles out of her as she finally releases Madison. "Well, that last girl you brought home—"

Jackson quirks an eyebrow, cutting her off.

"You should've seen her, Ky. Nothing but tattoos and titties!"

Jackson laughs.

They carry on talking about the girl—the girl I've never met. Would probably never meet. They have inside jokes—ones that I'll never know. Christine smiles sadly at me as if she somehow senses what I'm thinking.

It's not that I'm jealous, or mad even. I'm just *sorry*.

"Are those for me?" Christine asks, nodding to the forgotten lilies in my hand.

I try to smile, but I can't. "Yeah," I say, handing them to her. It all seems so stupid now—sending her anonymous flowers once a month. It wasn't enough. I had five years of catching up to do. Five years of inside jokes to make up for. And I swore it now—I'd start today.

She ignores the flowers and gives me a quick sideways hug. "I've missed you, Kyler."

CHRISTINE TAKES A liking to Madison right away—of course, I knew she would. Madison—she's kind of impossible not to like. But there's something off with Christine. She seems nervous and apprehensive. She often starts to speak and then cuts herself off. She can barely hold my gaze. I give Jackson a questioning look, but he just shrugs.

JAX AND I sit at the kitchen counter while Christine shows Madison how to bake Jax's and my favorite cookies from when we were kids. Madison pays attention to the details, even going as far as writing down the recipe. Jackson rolls his eyes at them. Madison fakes a glare his direction. "It's important I know this stuff," she tells him. "How else am I going to keep him?"

MADISON

"HOW LONG HAVE you known Ky?" Christine asks, motioning to what I assume is Ky's childhood bed. I look over my shoulder, half hoping Ky will show up and save me from the conversation I know I'm about to have.

"Not long." I sit on the bed and bite my lip, my hands clasped on my lap as I look around Ky's old bedroom. Having Ky by my side was comforting, but now I'm alone. And if Christine's anything like Ky says she is, I'm about to cop a ton of questions. Most likely ones about whether or not I'm good enough for Ky. I'm not. I know that. Which I guess is the reason why I'm so damn nervous.

"Did he tell you about me?" she asks.

"Yes," I manage to say.

"What did he say?"

"That you were badass and that I remind him of you a little..."

She laughs—this all-consuming laugh that has me relaxing slightly. After a moment, she sighs and sits down on the bed next to me. "I've missed him," she says, like it's something she hasn't been able to admit before.

"I bet," I tell her. "I'd miss him, too, if he were gone that long. Hell, I miss him when he's not right next to me."

She reaches over, taking my hand in hers and settling them between us. I almost flinch, not used to the comfort it gives me. Her touch is soft, warm—everything a mother's should be. My chest tightens, memories of my own mother trying to break free.

I don't let it happen. I can't.

"I'm holding on to a lot of secrets," she says. "And I don't think I'm ready to face them."

"About Ky?" I ask, turning to her.

She wipes tears off her cheeks and nods, releasing a silent sob as she does.

"Secrets aren't good..." *Trust me*, I want to say. *I would know.* "Especially with Ky. Whatever you're keeping from him, he deserves to know. He cares so much about you," I add. "We wouldn't be here if he didn't."

Her smile reaches her eyes as she tilts her head to the side. "Young lady, I think he wouldn't be here if he didn't care about *you*."

I stay silent.

"Do you care about him?" she asks.

More than I should. I push down the sob and nod. "Yes," I tell her, looking her right in the eyes. "Actually, I think I'm in love with him."

KY

"WHAT DID MOM whisper to you when I went to get Madison?" I ask Jackson, eyeing the doorway that Mom and Maddy just walked through, hoping they can't hear us.

He laughs. "That Madison was smokin' hot."

"And you agreed?"

"Dude, have you *seen* Madison?"

"I've seen more of her than you ever will, asshole."

"Yeah, but I can still get off imagining it," he says through a chuckle.

I punch his arm.

He doesn't even flinch.

"What do you press these days?" I ask, shaking out my hand to relieve the pain.

"What? Are you jealous?"

I shrug. "A little."

"I'm not that kid anymore, Ky."

"You're just avoiding my question. Tell me."

He shakes his head and changes the subject. "You need to speak to Mom."

"Yeah, I know. Is she acting strange right now?" *Or maybe I just don't know her anymore*, I think.

"She carries a lot of guilt, Ky, and you're the only one that can fix that."

"Guilt over what?"

"Talk to her."

It's silent a moment, my mind reeling with so many thoughts I can't focus on one.

Jax clears his throat, bringing me back to reality. "So, four days."

I turn to him, confusion clear on his face.

"The fight?"

"Yeah." I sigh.

He glances around the room, making sure we're still alone. "And you haven't heard from DeLuca?"

"Nope. He said he'd be out of town, though."

"He did?" he asks, surprise clear in his tone.

I eye him sideways. "Yeah... why?"

"My guys have been tailing him. He hasn't gone anywhere."

"What?"

"Why the hell would he lie to you?"

"I have no idea."

Madison's sniffle interrupts us. She walks into the room wiping her cheeks, Christine behind her. "You broke her, Ma," I tease, pulling Madison to my side. "You okay? What happened?"

She kisses me quickly but stays silent.

"Kyler," Christine says, her voice shaking. "Can we talk?"

* * *

WE TAKE THE fresh cookies out onto the back patio. Jackson grabs two handfuls of them, lifts the bottom of his shirt, and uses it to store them. Then he grabs Madison's hand and leads her away, giving Christine and me the alone time we both need. "Let me show you around the yard," Jax jokes, pointing his finger at a bush. "This bush right here is called the Sophia. Named after *the* Sophia Bush. Latin name, the Jaxjerkoffagus."

Madison's head throws back with her laugh. "I have no idea who Sophia Bush is."

Jackson glares at her, then at me, then back at her with a look of disgust. "I need to talk to Kylie about his choice of girls." He shakes his head at her. "Sophia Bush is the hottest girl who's ever existed." He gives her a quick once-over. "You actually look a lot like her."

Madison grins from ear-to-ear. "You think I'm hot?"

His eyes widen. "Moving on," he says loudly.

Christine and I settle on the patio furniture, watching them. Madison laughs again, placing her hand in the crook of his elbow. He smiles down at her before walking to the next plant. "This one here," he says, faking a posh British accent, "is the Tyra, a form of banksia. Named after Tyra Banks, of course. Latin name—"

"Let me guess," Madison cuts in. "The Jaxbeatoffalot."

He barks out a guffaw. "No, young Madison," he says, patting the top of her head gently. "Nice try. It's called the Jaxspankbanksimus."

I turn to the sound of Christine laughing next to me. She's watching them, but I need her to *see* me. "Ma?"

She tenses. "Yes, sweetheart?"

"You wanted to talk?"

She pushes her shoulders back, gearing herself up for what she's going to say next. I find myself copying her, choosing to ignore the thumping of my heart. Then she looks at me with those eyes so familiar, and everything else fades away. "I'm sorry, Ky."

Confusion blurs my mind. "Why are you sorry? I'm the one who left."

She swallows, fighting back the tears threatening to fall. "I'm the one who let you."

"Ma—"

"No. I've waited five years for this conversation, Kyler. I have it memorized, so please let me get it out."

I nod, the lump in my throat refusing to let me speak.

"I was meant to be your mother. Your rock. But I failed you. When Jeff died—"

"Ma—"

She holds up her hand and continues. "When Jeff died, I should've been there for you. I was so consumed by my own loss that I didn't think about you boys. I didn't see how much you were suffering, and then Steven... I should've paid better attention—should've taken better care of you, Ky. Do you hear me?"

Her gaze holds mine while I clear my throat. "Yes, ma'am."

"You were just a kid. You were hurt and lost and *desperate*. I shouldn't have let you leave... and when you did—"

"You didn't know," I cut in.

"I knew where you were stationed, Ky. I knew when you deployed."

"Then why didn't you call me?"

"Because I was guilt-stricken and I was ashamed, Ky. And when my friends would ask me how you were, I told them you were great—that I sent you packages often. How insane is that? I was lying to everyone, and I was lying to myself."

"Ma, you can't blame yourself. You were going through the same thing. I chose to leave you behind. You and Jackson—you needed me and I just left."

"But you were suffering more than just the loss of Jeff and

your brother. You were *heartbroken...* and I wasn't there for you."

"You knew?"

She shakes her head. "Not at first. Jackson found out at school, and he told me—and even then I couldn't bring myself to care about anyone but myself."

"Come on, Ma," I comfort.

She wipes her eyes. "Thank God for Jackson," she says, looking over at them.

I follow her gaze. Jackson's throwing handfuls of dirt from the garden toward my old house while spewing immature profanities. "You piece of shit on a stick!"

Madison's holding her stomach from laughing so hard.

"Yeah," I say, "Thank God for Jackson."

He throws another handful. "You shit stinking whore face!"

Madison laughs harder.

"You try it," Jax says, dropping dirt in her palms.

"Try what?"

"Just yell whatever you've always wanted to and throw the dirt."

Madison looks at the dirt in her hands, then back up at Jax.

"Seriously," he encourages. "It feels *so* good."

Madison nods, a slow smirk developing. Then, as loud as she can, she yells, "You child-abusing, alcoholic, dick of a cunt!"

* * *

WE LEAVE SOON after Madison dropped the C bomb. Christine pretty much declared her love for Madison right then and there. Jackson, too. But to be honest, I passed that stage a long time ago.

We spend the car ride home feeding Madison stories from when we were kids, and it feels good—better than good—to be able to sit back and laugh about the good times instead of just remembering the bad. Because there actually wasn't that much of it—bad, I mean.

And Madison—she's living proof of that.

It took Madison coming into my life for me to let go of the past, of the guilt that I've carried with me since the day Jeff died. How can you thank someone for giving you that gift —the gift of being able to *breathe* again?

I'M QUIET AS we take the elevator up to our floor after Jackson drops us off. I can see her watching me—waiting for me to say something. I don't, because I *can't*.

We stay silent as we walk into my apartment and she steps in behind me, apprehensively closing the door. "Ky," she starts, then breaks off when I turn to her, my gaze pinning her in place. "If you're mad at me for overstepping, get it out now. I'd rather you yell at me than not talk to me again." She chews her lip, her gaze lowering.

Say something. "Madison." It's all I can say. *'Thank you'* doesn't do her justice. *'I love you'*—well, it's pretty damn close. I take the few steps to get to her and then lift her chin with my finger.

The tears in her eyes cloak the uncertainty behind them.

Her chest rises when mine falls.

She exhales.

I inhale.

She takes.

I give.

She pushes out a breath.

I pull one in.

So here we are—taking each other's *breaths* away.

MY GAZE DROPS to her mouth; her bottom lip quivers

with each release, and I look back into her eyes. "Ky?" Her voice echoes in my mind, playing havoc with my heart.

It's just like her knocks.

Quiet.

Timid.

And then it happens—the final gasp of breath before I can no longer breathe without her knowing the truth. "I..." *Love you.* Say it!

I can't. But I don't have to.

"I know," she whispers. "I do, too."

Our mouths crash together, frantic at first, and then after a beat... *imperfectly perfect.* My body covers hers, my hands everywhere all at once. And then, in sync, we slow down.

Maybe we both know that this isn't like the other times. We aren't driven by lust or by our physical need to be together.

This is so much more.

More than I ever expected.

And I know it now—that I was wrong.

I wasn't waiting for *her* to be ready.

She was waiting for me.

And I'm finally ready to give her everything.

I pull away, intent on telling her how I feel.

But the words are caught—not in my throat—but in my heart.

So I do the next best thing. I place my hand on her chest, covering her heart. And when she looks up at me, her eyes wide and waiting, I whisper, "Madison, I *exist* in here."

MADISON

I CAN'T RECALL ever seeing magic. Not in person and not on TV. So it made me wonder how I knew what it was or how it was supposed to make me feel.

But when Ky Parker places his palm on my chest—holding my heart in his hand—I somehow knew.

I felt it.

Magic.

And magic, at least for me, was undeniably, unequivocally, real.

27

KY

SHE TAKES MY hand and leads me to the bedroom—the same room where we've spent so many nights together, but we both know that tonight's different.

It's the beginning of a new existence.

She sits on the edge of the bed, her hands twisting on her lap. "I'm scared," she says.

I sit next to her. "Of what?"

"Everything." She turns to me. "I'm scared of *feeling* too much... of *wanting* too much."

I watch as tears pool in her eyes and she tries to breathe through it, but the air's too thick. I know—because I feel it, too.

I reach up to cup her face, my thumb wiping at her tears. "You have no reason to be scared, Maddy." I kiss her once. "I'm not going anywhere."

Her eyes flick between mine, carrying an emotion I can't decipher. We stay that way, a thousand unanswered questions between us. But none of them matter. Not to me—and not to her—because when she leans forward and captures my mouth with hers, we become lost in the moment and in each other.

I gently push on her shoulders until she's on her back and I'm resting on my elbows, looking down on her. Kissing her. Feeling her. Wanting her. *Needing her.*

My hand drifts down her body, past her breasts, her hips, and down her thighs until I feel the hem of her dress. Then I move up under the material and onto the softness of her thighs until my fingers meet the lace of her panties. She reaches down, pulling on my shirt, asking for permission.

I sit up slightly, just enough for her to pull it over my head and then I'm back, my mouth on hers and my hands between her legs, moving her panties to the side. A gasp escapes her when my finger slides effortlessly inside. Her back arches, causing her head to tilt back, away from our kiss. So I kiss her jaw, her neck, her shoulder, down to her chest—the entire time my finger causing her to moan, to grip the covers beneath her. "Ky..."

I kiss each breast, over her dress, and move down her stomach. Her fingers lace through my hair, her body writhing beneath me.

I stand up and remove my jeans and boxers in one swift move. Then I remain at the side of the bed and eye her from head-to-toe. "Your turn."

She sits up on her knees and smiles. "You do it."

I smile back, taking a step forward and slowly lifting her dress over her head and then removing her bra. I lean down, taking her nipple into my mouth while my thumb skims over the other. She pushes me away after a long moment and scoots back on the bed so her head's resting on a pillow. "I need you."

"You'll have me," I assure her, "as soon as I finish worshipping you." I climb between her legs again, where I plan on finishing what I started. Her fingers find my hair the same time my tongue finds her clit.

"Oh God..."

I flatten my tongue at her entrance and do something I know drives her insane. Slowly, softly, I lick all the way from the bottom to the top.

She pants, her hips thrusting, matching the sounds. I reach up and push a single finger into her. "Ky!"

I pull out my finger, replace it with two, and match the rhythm of her thrusts. "Stop," she pants. "Please. It's too much... I can't... I'm going... *fuck*!"

Her hips lift, her fingers gripping my hair tighter. Her thighs tense... "Oh...oh...OH!" She moans through every single wave of her orgasm. "Holy shit." Then she collapses, her phenomenal breasts heaving as she tries to catch her breath, her entire body covered in a sheen of sweat. I kiss her mound one more time before making my way up, wiping my mouth as I do. Then I kiss her stomach, each breast, and all the way up her neck and to her ear, my cock resting at her entrance. "Are you sure, Maddy?"

Her hands run down the center of my back and rest on my hips. She doesn't respond with words, but she raises her hips and grips mine, pulling me inside her.

My mouth clamps around her shoulder, muffling the moan that escapes me, then I lean up on my elbows, resting them on either side of her head. Her eyes lock on my lips as she licks hers. Then she leans up, pressing her tongue against my lips. I open my mouth for her, reveling in the feel of her tongue against mine, tasting her own pleasure.

I pull back quickly. "Condom," I pant. "Shit, I forgot." I start to pull out but she stops me.

"I'm protected."

My gaze flicks between her eyes and her lips. "Are you sure?"

She nods.

I pull almost all the way out, and then I slowly push back in.

Her eyes roll before they close.

So I do it again.

And again.

And again.

I keep doing it until her whispers of my name turn to moans and I can no longer hold out.

And then she says it. "I love you, Kyler."

And I fall over the edge.

Physically.

Emotionally.

And wholeheartedly.

28

KY

I SIT ON the couch after training the next morning, phone in hand.

Madison and I spent the entire night naked and in each other's arms. She fell asleep right away. I stayed up most of the night, lost in a sea of my own thoughts.

I was still like that when I fumbled my way through this morning's sparring session. She'd sent me a text and told me she was at Debbie's and would be home about an hour after I got here. And for the first time since I met her, I'm grateful she isn't around.

I stare at Jackson's number, palms sweaty and heart racing at the thought of how he'll react to what I'm about to tell him. I flake out at the last second and dial Christine's number instead. She answers, but she doesn't speak.

"Ma?"

"I just wanted to hear you say it again," she says, and I can actually hear the smile in her voice. "How are you, Ky?"

I sigh loudly and rest my head on the back of the couch.

"What's wrong?" she asks.

"How do you know something's wrong?"

"Kyler."

I clear my throat. "I'm in love, Ma."

"No shit."

I laugh.

"So... what's the problem?" she asks.

I swallow down the knot in my throat; the revelation of the truth feels like a vice surrounding my heart. "I don't feel worthy of *her*, or *love,* in general."

"Shut up, Ky!"

"Ma—"

"No. You listen, and you listen good. I will not let you sit there and talk nonsense. Do you hear me?" Her voice is strained, like she's holding back tears. "I will not listen to you talk about yourself like that. After everything you've been though, Kyler, that night when you fell through my back door, bleeding and pleading for help... I thank God every day that you chose me. That you let me help you, because Lord knows you needed help. Those people that raised you—those monsters—they'll rot in hell for what they did, for the way they treated that poor, poor boy you used to be. How you—" She chokes on a sob but recovers quickly. "How you got out alive... I'll never know. But fate was on your side, and on ours, and you became a blessing in all our lives. So don't you dare —" Another sob. "Don't you dare ever, *ever*," she grinds out, "believe that you aren't worthy of every great possibility this world has to offer. And Madison—she sees that. And she appreciates you for everything that you are. And she loves you for everything that you've accomplished and the man you've turned out to be." She pauses to take a few calming breaths. "Don't live in the past, Kyler; dream about the future. You and Madison—you can *have* a future. You can have it all."

"Like you and Jeff?" I whisper.

"Better. Because you, more than anyone, know how

quickly life can change. You'll know not to take it for granted. Every sense. Every step. Every breath, Ky. There's so much of everything—"

"And all I have to do is exist," I finish for her.

She laughs through her tears. "Yes, Ky. Exactly."

"I love you, Ma."

"I love you, too, son."

"I'll come by soon, okay?"

"You bring that girl of yours with you."

"Of course. It's hard to be without her."

I STARE AT my phone long after we hang up. Then I blow out a heavy breath—Christine's words the final push I need to gain the courage.

I call Jackson.

"You okay?" he says in greeting.

"Yeah..." I settle my hand on my knee to stop it from bouncing uncontrollably. "Actually, no," I admit.

"What's going on? Are you hurt?"

"No, I'm fine," I say quickly.

I hear him release what I assume is a relieved breath.

"But I did want to talk to you, and I just want you to hear me out."

"Okay?"

Rubbing my eyes, I curse under my breath.

"Just say it, Ky."

"Remember how you said that if I ever wanted out, to say the word?"

"Yeah?"

"Word."

Silence.

Followed by more silence.

I stand quickly, my head spinning from the sudden movement.

"Say something, Jax."

"I'm coming over."

TEN MINUTES LATER he shows up, loosening his tie as he walks through my door. "Where's Madison?" he asks, searching for her.

"She's working over at Debbie's Flowers."

"Beer?"

"Fridge. Aren't you on duty?"

"Fuck it."

I move to the kitchen and rest against the counter opposite him while he pulls out a beer from the fridge and takes a swig, his eyes never leaving mine. When he's done, he swallows loudly and crosses his arms. "Is this about Madison? Does she know?"

"No! Of course not. I wouldn't tell her."

"So?"

I shrug.

He rubs his hand across his face, then places the beer on the counter. "You want to know why I became a cop?"

I nod.

"Because of you, Ky."

"What?"

"Because I wanted to find a way to protect kids in the same situation as you. I wanted to find a way to ruin the people who think it's okay to beat on defenseless kids. I wanted to take them down. Destroy them." He clears his throat before adding, "You were my best friend, Ky, and then you became my brother. Maybe you didn't see it—or maybe I didn't let it show—but your pain, your anguish, your anger—I felt all of that."

"Jax, it wasn't your burden to carry."

"You think you'd be saying that if it were the other way around?"

"No."

He pushes off the counter and starts to pace. "You know at the beginning, I had this vendetta... child abusers, molesters, traffickers, I wanted to ruin them all. And I did. For a while... and it felt good, you know? I felt like I was making a difference. And I felt like, somehow, I was getting justice for you. Wherever the hell you were in the world, I felt like I was making you proud."

I keep my head down so he won't see the tears welling in my eyes.

He sniffs, then lets a chuckle escape him. "And then, I don't know... maybe I lost my way. Maybe I felt like it wasn't enough. So I started looking up the night Steve died—for you, Ky. Because I wanted that for *you*. That closure—or revenge—or whatever the fuck you want to call it. I became a detective so I could get closer to the case. So I could find the people responsible."

I inhale deeply and finally face him. He's still pacing, his head lowered. "Maybe it's not important to you—and I get that—"

"Of course it's important," I cut in. "But will it change anything? No. No one put a gun to Steve's head and made him take it."

Jax stops in his tracks, his eyes snapping to mine.

"Don't get me wrong. I appreciate what you did, what you *do*, who you *are*..." My shoulders slump with my sigh. "I just need to move on, Jax. And maybe you do, too. I need to stop living there—in the past—holding on to the same guilt and regret I've felt for the last five years. I want to move forward."

"So you're done?"

I shake my head. "I'll fight tomorrow, see what I can find out about the actual night you think the handover will happen. If I find anything and it leads us somewhere, then no, I won't be done. I just need to know there's an end in sight. I can't do this forever. It's not fair on me or—"

"Madison?" he cuts in, eyebrows raised.

I nod.

"I don't know what to say, Ky."

"You're mad?"

"No."

"Disappointed?"

"No."

"Then what?"

"I'm kind of in shock."

"What?"

The front door opens and Madison steps in. Neither of us greets her. We're too busy focusing on each other. She comes up next to me and kisses my cheek. "Hey, babe."

"Hey," I reply, finally switching my attention to her. "How was work?"

"It was good." She glances at Jackson quickly. "Did I interrupt something?"

"No," Jax says, backing away from us. "Did I hear it's your birthday soon, Maddy?"

She shakes her head, her eyes narrowed as she looks between us. "No. Not until April."

"Oh yeah?" Jax asks. "Sixteenth, right?"

"No. Twenty-third." She looks back at me. "Why?"

"Ky was trying to organize a trip as a surprise. He said he didn't know when your birthday was—thought I'd save him the embarrassment of asking you." Jackson fakes a laugh, though Madison wouldn't know it's fake. "I'll let myself out. You guys have a good night."

29

KY

I TWIST A strand of Madison's hair that's lying over my chest while we lay in bed. "So I have something I need to do tomorrow night," I say, trying to be as casual as possible.

"Oh yeah? Where are we going?"

"Yeah. About that... you can't come."

She tilts her head and looks up at me, eyebrows drawn. "Why not?"

"You know all that training I've been doing?"

"Yeah?"

"So... don't get mad, but I'm fighting tomorrow. Like, in an organized event."

"Why?" she asks, more out of curiosity than anger.

I shrug and give her a half-truth. "I just want to see if I'm any good."

"So why can't I go with you?"

"Because you'd be a distraction. I wouldn't be able to concentrate knowing you were there watching me, worried about me. And that doesn't even count the amount of times I'd be looking over at you making sure no assholes were making moves on you."

She smiles, but it's sad. "Do you have to?"

"It's not a big deal, Maddy. It's all legit. They have doctors—"

"No," she cuts it. "That's not—" She kisses my chest before looking up at the ceiling. "Never mind. I just don't want anything to happen to you."

I kiss the top of her head. "I promise you, nothing will happen. I'll tap out as soon as I feel the need. Like I said, it's not about the victory or whatever... I'm just curious."

"Just make sure you come out alive, okay?"

* * *

I DON'T GO TOO HARD AT TRAINING in the morning so I can rest up for the fight. I'd love to say that I'm confident about the win, but after researching James Hayden online, I know I have a decent fight on my hands.

But the fight isn't what's making me anxious—it's my word to Jackson. I'll do what I can to find out as much information as possible. Truthfully, I want to find something, anything that's substantial enough for Jackson to use. Then we'd both be happy—or at the least, satisfied.

* * *

MADISON LOOKS UP from behind the counter of Debbie's Flowers when I step in, a huge smile on her face. She straightens her arms on the counter and pushes up, her eyes closed and lips puckered and waiting. I wipe the sweat off my face and make my way over to her, kissing her quickly—just once. Then I go in for another, and another, and another and when I pull back, her smile's still in place. "Another one?" she asks.

"Hey! That's my line."

She laughs.

I give her another one.

"You want to see what I've been working on?" she asks, rocking on her heels.

"Of course." I drop my gym bag and wait while she goes to the back room, and I take the time to check my phone.

Jackson: Call me. It's urgent.

She returns a second later holding something behind her back.

"Ready?"

"For you? Always."

"Ta da!" she says, revealing a bouquet of flowers. Half white lilies, half Madisons. "You like?"

"I love."

"You think Christine will like them? I'm getting them delivered to her."

"Really?" I can't help but smile. "You don't have to do that."

With a shrug, she says, "I want to." Then she reaches behind the counter for a pen, just as Debbie appears from the storeroom.

"Oh good, Kyler's here," she sings. She rises to her toes and picks up an old Polaroid camera from the shelf behind the counter.

"They still make those?" I ask her.

"Nothing will ever replace instant memories," she says.

She stands behind the counter and fiddles with it while mumbling, "We can send a picture of you two holding it when it gets delivered. It's more personal that way. This damn thing..."

I chuckle as Madison wraps her arm around my waist. "You're sticky and smelly," she whispers.

"And you love it," I tease.

She scrunches her nose.

"Okay!" Debbie shouts like we're in another room. "Make it a good one," she says, lifting the camera to her eye.

I look down at Madison, but she's already watching me, contentment in her eyes that I'm sure matches mine.

I feel like a teenager experiencing love for the first time. Like the world has never shown me an ounce of sadness or regret. Madison—she makes everything feel like the first time. "I love you," she mouths.

"I love you, too," I say, before I close my eyes, lean down and press my lips to hers.

I hear the bell above the door chime.

The click-whoosh of the Polaroid camera.

Then Debbie's gasp, followed by a deathly shriek.

My eyes shoot open and snap to her, but she's no longer standing there. She's sitting behind the counter, knees raised and her hands covering her head, shielding herself.

My heart stops. "Debbie?"

"Oh my God," Madison whispers, and I turn to her quickly. She's facing the front of the store, all color drained from her face.

I follow her gaze.

"Nate," she whispers, just as he comes into my vision.

But the man before me isn't the Nate DeLuca I've always seen.

There's no calm in his eyes.

No intimidation in his stance.

His cap's pulled low, his hoodie covering it.

His arms are at his sides, one hand loosely gripping his gun.

I pull Madison behind me, my heart thumping against my chest.

DeLuca steps closer, wiping his face with his sleeve.

I think it's sweat, but the closer he comes, the clearer I see him.

His body shakes, his hand trembling as he wipes at the tears filling his eyes.

I hear Tiny's voice. "Boss Man, *don't* do this."

Madison's grip on the back of my shirt tightens.

She lets out a sob.

DeLuca's movements are slow.

Or so it seems.

Then he lifts the pistol, aimed at my head, and takes the final steps to get to me.

I should move.

I should do something.

Anything.

He's two feet in front of me now, his gun still pointed.

His chest heaves with each shaky breath.

Inhale.

Exhale.

Madison releases my shirt, and I feel her move next to me.

His gaze switches to her.

He blinks.

Once.

Twice.

Then he speaks.

"Get in the fucking car, Bailey."

Jackson: *It's Madison.*
Jackson: *She's not who she says she is.*

EPILOGUE

I REFUSE TO look at Dr. Aroma when I ask, "You said your parents were on crack?"

"Yes, I did say that."

"Were you serious?"

"No, Ky. It was a metaphor. They're just loopy."

"My parents were on crack. No metaphor." I uncross my arms and look around her office, my eyes catching on a framed picture of her in a graduation gown with an older couple. "They your parents?"

"Yes."

"I could have been you," I mumble.

"What do you mean?"

"I found my birth dad. He's straight edge. I could've gone to college, gotten a degree. I could have been you."

"And why don't you think you turned out that way?"

"Like I said, my parents were on crack."

"And it affected you how?"

"I'm allowed to be bitter, right?" I ask, ignoring her question.

"You're allowed to feel however you want to feel, Ky."

"As long as it's not angry?"

"What makes you say that?"

"Because it leads me here."

"To my office?"

"No." I look back at her. "To the edge of *destruction.*"

ABOUT THE AUTHOR

Jay McLean is an international best-selling author and full-time reader, writer of New Adult and Young Adult romance, and skilled procrastinator. When she's not doing any of those things, she can be found running after her three little boys, investing way too much time on True Crime Documentaries and binge-watching reality TV.

She writes what she loves to read, which are books that can make her laugh, make her hurt and make her feel.

Jay lives in the suburbs of Melbourne, Australia, in her dream home where music is loud and laughter is louder.

For publishing rights (Foreign & Domestic) Film or television, please contact her agent Erica Spellman-Silverman, at Trident Media Group.

Made in the USA
Columbia, SC
06 October 2020